HEARTLAND STORIES OF THE SOUTHWEST

HEARTLAND
STORIES
OF THE
SOUTHWEST

Rubén Darío Sálaz

Santa Fe, New Mexico

WORKS BY RUBEN DARIO SALAZ

Tierra Amarilla Shootout
Cosmic: The La Raza Sketchbook
Cosmic Posters (bilingual)
The Cosmic Reader of the Southwest — for Young People
Indian Saga Posters
Le lectura cósmica del Suroeste — para los jóvenes
Heartland Stories of the Southwest

Cover photograph by Fred Patton

Manufactured in The United States of America
Blue Feather Press
P.O. Box 5113, Santa Fe, N.M.
87502

For my wife,
Maria Magdalena
MYDA

Valentine pumpkin
of the midnight mountains,
Living velvet and sourcream silence,
Laughing melodies and bathtub earmuffs,
the dawn of our awakening.

CONTENTS

FOREWARD

by W. G. Shrubsall
(formerly of the University of Kentucky)

I wish this volume had been available when I moved to New Mexico in 1969. This date, by historical standards, makes me a newcomer to New Mexico. By some local standards, perhaps it makes me an intruder, one to be suspect because I am descended from Germans and Englishmen. Of course, this is a common refrain in many geographic regions in the United States of America; the tune is the same though the words change with the location. A popular song of twenty years ago says that "the French hate the Germans, the Germans hate the Poles, Italians hate Yugoslavs, South Africans hate the Dutch — and I don't like anybody very much." The human condition is too often sadly, and more often than not, accurately captured by these words.

So enter one more Anglo to the Southwestern stage. When I arrived, I was carefully taught to be watchful around the local Hispanics, who "hated," and were "hated by," the Anglos. This is what I was taught. But I have been around other cultural areas where such problems exist — or seem to, and so I knew that such hatred was probably a gross oversimplification of the truth. As I settled into the ways of New Mexico, I learned that I was right. There are numerous factors which lead to misunderstanding, and none of them can singly account for the problems confronting peoples of different backgrounds and cultures.

Rather than being outraged by the actions and beliefs of sects and peoples who did not quite swallow the "American Pie" attitude of melting-pot theorists, I became intrigued. I have found that so-called dissidents usually have cause in most cases, and that one cannot simply dismiss them as being troublemakers or chronic malcontents. It is the small-minded person who cannot see beyond a single event which shapes a mode of thought. It is the morally-lax individual who bases an attitude on prejudice alone and who will not attempt to examine all possible causes leading to conflict. Yet, this is the human condition, for most people cannot and will not take the time to look beyond the surface of their feelings and reactions; people have so acted from time immemorial.

Not so with Rubén Darío Sálaz. He has taken the time to examine the past and present factors concerning the Southwestern situation, and we — Hispanics, Anglos, Indians, Blacks, in short, all of us who reside in the Southwest — are the better for it.

Sálaz has written for most of his life about the Southwestern past, present, and future. One of his books, *Cosmic: the La Raza Sketchbook,* presented the Hispanic version of Southwestern history, and did it well. The book was reviewed enthusiastically and justified the very first Blue Feather Press Award. In clear, concrete terms, Sálaz depicted the Southwest as it was and is, especially to Hispanos.

In these stories of the *Heartland,* Sálaz has given the reader a fascinating selection of stories which are historic and modern, humorous and tragic, heroic and pathetic — but importantly, true. I do not mean that they are true only in the sense that eight of the ten stories are based upon factual episodes. Rather, the stories are true in that they capture the universal truth of the human condition while presenting localized plots, settings, lives and themes.

These stories follow the ancient artistic axiom, "to delight and to instruct." First, the stories are clearly written, and they incorporate a use of detail and characterization which cannot fail to move the most massive stone-heart. They are humorous, they are sad; they infuriate, they charm; they are good yarns, they are great drama.

And they instruct. Had I only read some of these when I first arrived in 1969, I would have been better prepared for the Southwestern experience. The problems of the Southwestern past which continue today are here: the animosity and blanket mistrust of "civilized" whites toward the Indian; the wastefulness of the encroaching Easterner; the disappearance of a simpler and more ecological, more satisfying way of life; the destruction of a basic morality by a nonexistent one. And the great themes of literature are found in these stories, too: the tragedy of the individual; the power of Darkness; the crassness of fate; the "machine in the garden;" and the loss of Eden.

Sálaz' greatest power may lie in the last of these themes. He is a Tolstoyian in that he laments the passing of the self-sufficient pastoral way of life common to the Southwest and in that he clearly questions the ugly, industrialized, federalized beast which devoured it. He is a humanitarian in that he is infuriated by the injustices perpetrated by the mindless individuals who intruded to destroy rather than to employ. And he is interested that *everyone* understand the Hispanic way, a culture which produced a working civilization for centuries, so that it may not perish in the electronic and mechanized and impersonal confusion of the modern era. *Heartland Stories of the Southwest* are a lasting contribution for newcomer and native alike. They will become a permanent light in Southwestern literature.

W. G. S.

I

THE RACE

Corporal George Daniel White of the U.S. Cavalry crouched low behind a protective craggy rock. He was sure he had heard a human voice just before his company of soldiers had been ambushed by the very Apaches the Army had been chasing. It was the same pattern: the murdering Apaches would attack or ambush at will, seemingly, then disappear as shadows in the desert. The soldiers pursued the hostiles at every opportunity but doing battle only with the sun, the heat, the thirsty sands, and barren mountains which seemed to swallow the Apaches without a trace. He was beginning to think it would be easier to bag the wild geese. How long had they been after the marauders led by Hosanna ... twenty days ... thirty? He wasn't sure anymore. But he was certain he had heard a voice, maybe that of a child, somewhere in the area, just before the ambush. When all hell broke loose he spurred his mount toward cover only to have it shot from under him. His fall could have been much worse, even if his head throbbed where he had rolled into a small boulder. His horse was already dead when White grabbed his rifle from the saddle scabbard and lay motionless in the rocks. He realized he should find his comrades and rejoin them but for the moment all his energy cried out for battle with the Apache enemy. Besides, the crack of a rifle was heard to reverberate every so often, clashing with the wild mountain peaks, telling him the soldiers couldn't be too far away. If he could only get an Apache! He knew the hostiles had their women and children with them ... that *had* to slow them down ... but he hadn't even caught a glimpse of them yet ... this was it ... now ... if he could only get his hands on an Apache! He had been among those chosen at Fort Huachuca because he was among the best athletes in the Army. Today he would do his share to put an end to Apache murder and pillage.

White turned toward the echo of a lingering rifle shot but he couldn't see anyone. None of his comrades were in sight and he knew better than to expect to see an Apache. He wasn't a veteran of the Indian wars but neither was he a raw recruit. He waited and continued to scrutinize the terrain ... perhaps he hadn't heard anything after all ... maybe one of the horses had made the sound ... maybe his imagination was playing tricks with his weary state and — *there it was again!* He was certain of it now ... the wail of a small child! So one of the Apaches had hidden his brats while he took the cavalry on tour, eh? Well, it wasn't going to work this time!

The revelation gave the soldier a new determination. In his enthusiasm he forgot the endless hours in the saddle, the odious hard-tack and salt horse, the ghastly barren mountains and the fearful lifeless sands of the desert. The savage enemies of his country were no longer specks on the horizon, no longer murderous shadows. His skill had discovered them and his superiority would exterminate them.

White crawled ever so carefully in the direction of the wail. Exactly where was the hiding place? He didn't want to stumble into it, not with Apaches there. One thing was sure, he didn't want to be taken alive by any Apaches. The memory of the last raid was still vivid: the ranchhouse bare and blackened, the carcasses of a dozen cattle scattered here and yonder. Even worse, stretched on the cruel sand was the owner of the ranch: a stake, cut from his own wagon, was driven through his stomach and deep into the earth. The eyeballs had been gouged out of their sockets and replaced wrong-side out. His ears had been pinned with cactus thorns to the sides of his nose. But these barbarities were minor compared to those suffered by the rancher's wife. When he saw how ... he had become sick ... and an Apache hater forever. No, he would never be taken alive by Apaches and he would never take any of them alive either.

"What are you doing thinking about being captured?" White thought to himself almost angrily. *"The other boys are around here someplace ... they'll be back and mebbe they'll have Hosanna with 'em. No stinking 'paches are ever gonna take me ... I'm doing the taking."*

George White of the U.S. Cavalry wasn't merely indulging himself. He was an excellent soldier and he knew something about fighting Apaches. It could be said with all truthfulness that he was the flower of the Army: blond, six-foot-three, sunburned, two-hundred-thirteen pounds of powerful, knotted muscles. He was handpicked for this expedition because of his abilities and willingness to combat the Apache enemy. He had learned that Apaches valued courage more than anything else and he respected their fighting ability but he knew their days were numbered because they stood in the way of progress. He exuded confidence as an athlete, a fighter, a soldier. He knew his weapons, the product of a superior civilization, were better than those used by the Apaches and he realized his army was larger than all the renegade Apache bands put together. The hostile Apache was little more than a murderous corpse who would soon be rotting in a grave or in jail. White would win, it could turn out in no other way.

The soldier lost all track of time as he crawled this way and that in a concentrated effort to find his adversaries. As the sun was beginning to set he heard the same wailing sound directly to his right. While nothing was visible he knew that right behind what seemed to be nothing more than a large craggy rock was a nest of Apaches. The entrance to what must be some sort of a small cave in the side of the mountain was on the opposite side because all White could see was solid rock. He squinted into the setting sun. It would be dark soon: should he surprise them right away? The nest probably wasn't concealing any men. They were making shadows for the benefit of the cavalry, away from the women and children . . . but they had to come back for them. He would camouflage himself as well as possible and wait in hopes of killing one or two warriors from Hosanna's band. Besides, his head was throbbing and some rest would help. The Apaches in the cave couldn't leave without him knowing it.

The desert night set in with silence and moon splashings contrasted by shadows. White made his way back where his horse lay, ate what little food remained in his saddle bags and drank from his near empty canteen. He took the bags off the horse and hunted for a protected place where he could rest without being seen by intruders and still be able to watch the cave area. He considered himself divinely redeemed when he encountered a space under an overhanging peak of jutting rock. He went in on his knees but froze when he heard the warning whir of death from a rattlesnake. White put his rifle out in front of him though he knew he couldn't use it and continue to keep his presence a secret from the Apaches. When he felt some pressure on the rifle barrel he instinctively withdrew the rifle and hurled his saddle bags at the snake. An eternity of ten seconds went by until he thought he heard a faint hum as the enemy dragged itself away. When he saw the snake wiggle across a slit of moonlight he waited a few seconds more then crawled into the disputed refuge. White felt a sharp sting on his forearm and was panic stricken for the briefest instant until he saw the emerald dagger of the amole plant was his antagonist, not the rattler. He composed himself and settled down to rest on the fine bed of sand. The soldier hoped the Apaches hadn't heard the noise of his crashing saddle bags as he peered at the vicinity of the enemy cave. No, there was no activity showing. He took a drink from his canteen, holding it in his mouth before swallowing. He was certain his lack of water would not become critical since his comrades would surely return tomorrow.

George White slept soundly in his sanctuary. Just before sunrise he awakened with a start and realized he would have been easy prey for any returning enemy. But he hadn't been discovered and now he was no longer bone-weary nor was his head throbbing anymore. Should he attack or wait? The mountains were deathly quiet. Where were his fellow soldiers? The Apache warriors? He was out of food, almost out of water, help was not in sight. Better attack immediately.

White left his saddle bags where they were and inched his way to the enemy cave. He used the gray-green sagebrush for camouflage as he avoided the bayonets of the aloe and trampled the blood-red blotches of the nopal and the snow-white marguerites. When he was close to the cave he looked around once more. There was absolutely no sound in the whole world of the desert. He cocked his rifle ever so slowly yet the death entering the chamber seemed to scream out in the stillness of the sunrise. He peered at the small entrance of the cave ... no one was visible ... he would have to shoot from a kneeling position ... crouched to his knees ... to his feet ... deep breath ... and charged!

The soldier's presence at the opening of the cave took the Apache woman and her two children by surprise but the Apache was trying to strike at the soldier as two bullets penetrated her chest. The bigger child connected with a rock just before a bullet crashed through its skull. The wailing of the youngest Apache stopped with an abrupt crack of the soldier's carbine.

White made certain the three Apaches were dead, after which he pulled out his knife and scalped them in order to collect the bounty which was on the head of every hostile Apache in the territory. When finished he looked around for something to eat, knowing that Apaches had caches of food, water, and ammunition all over the lands they roamed. He found nothing. He then ransacked the corpses in an effort to uncover the money which it was said Apaches always had. He found nothing as he became aware of a throbbing ache in his head where he had been hit on entering the cave. He sat down and collected his thoughts on getting back to Fort Huachuca. Finally he peered out of the cave, still very cautious, and realized he was not completely certain as to which direction to take for the fort. He believed it was ... due west. He was ready to exit when he thought he saw something moving about three hundred yards away. His eyebrows lowered as his eyelids narrowed in complete concentration ... where did it go? ... there, behind the craggy rock formation, an Apache, a man, heading toward the cave. White lifted his rifle then lowered the barrel. What if there were other warriors behind him? The soldier knew he could kill one more Apache but he also realized he was trapped in the cave if other Apaches blocked the entrance. If he was captured he would die a hideous death ... he focused his gun sight on the stalking Apache ... one shot is all he would need ... or get ... one reflection from the gun barrel meant detection ... the Apache was as near to death ...

Suddenly White saw a faint glimmer for his own salvation. The Apache, marked for death by the V of the gunsight, would certainly know the way back to Fort Huachuca. *"I've gotta take him alive,"* he realized. White's blue eyes narrowed to slits. The Apache would be at the cave within a couple of minutes. The soldier saw his own boot tracks outside. *"I gotta distract him!"* He looked down at the dead Apaches, dragged the older boy and laid his arm out by the entrance, hoping the arm would attract the Apache's attention before the boot prints screamed out their warning. White went to the side of the cave and prepared to club the Apache as he came in. *"He must be close ... close to my trail ... where is he? ... why doesn't he come in? ... he knows something is wrong ... can he see the arm? ... God, the other bodies, can he see them? ... shoulda moved ... taking too long ... cry like the kid or it'll be too late!"* White uttered an almost indistinguishable sound that was enough to make the Apache enter the cave. He swung viciously at the long-haired head! The blow landed solidly and the Apache slumped into a heap. By instinct White turned the rifle around and almost sent some bullets into his enemy's skull but the unconscious Apache didn't move, thus saving his life. *"Tie him up, hurry. With what?!*" Then he remembered about the rawhide strips in his saddle bags. "*Go getem.*" He resisted the temptation of clubbing the unconscious Apache again just to make sure. "*What if there's more out there?*" He'd take his chances. He dashed out to the saddle bags, grabbed them and was quickly back at the cave, binding the Apache's limbs so tightly the circulation was nearly cut off. But White needn't have worried. The clout on the head kept the Apache unconscious for more than enough time for the soldier to regain his composure and confidence. There had been no other Apaches, obviously, and this one would lead White to Fort Huachuca or die. When the enemy opened its eyes the soldier was in complete control of himself and the situation. The savage tried to move but found he couldn't so he waited for the color to come back into the world. When it did he saw the remains of his family and a white soldier holding three trophies and grinning.

"Know what these are, 'pache?" asked White as he dangled the scalps in front of his foe. "If I didn't have plans for you I'd be holding yours too." The Apache tried to wrench himself free but all he accomplished for his effort was a kick in the stomach. "Don't tempt me!" spat White, "or your bones will be pickings for the vultures." White dragged the Apache outside and let him bathe in the sun. He drank the last of the water in his canteen and flung it away. "You and I, 'pache, are going to Huachuca, and when we get there we'll give you a fair trial and then take you out and hang you."

White looked in his saddlebags for anything he might want to take with him. The handcuffs, won in a poker game, were promptly snapped into place around the Apache's wrists after which White stuffed the key in his own pocket. He decided to take the binoculars, also part of his winnings, and the scalps, pistol, rifle, and knife.

"Huachuca, 'pach, you hear me?" said White as he pulled the Amerindian to his feet. "Fort Huachuca!" The soldier pushed the warrior who crashed to the ground because his ankles were still tightly bound. White sneered as he sat on him while he cut the rawhide. "Fort Huachuca!" he yelled as pulled the Apache to his feet by yanking on the long black hair.

White had no way of knowing his prisoner was Ulzana, the leader of the renegade Apaches the soldiers had been chasing. He couldn't know that was Ulzana's butchered family lying back there in the cave. He didn't realize Ulzana, not being born a chief, had achieved great fame in his tribe strictly through demonstrations of courage, cunning, and keenness on the warpath. He was unaware that his prisoner was the bloodiest and most sagacious of raiders.

The two men walked silently on the thirsty sands White had grown to hate. He looked around at the mountains as he walked: it was as if someone had thrown them down from the sky instead of growing naturally out of the earth. They looked dead, unkempt, craggy. Only the diabolic cactus was sharper than the crags and ragged peaks. "Don't lead me on no wild goose chase, 'pache," said a contemptuous White for he knew his guide didn't speak English except for place names. "Fort Huachuca, you savvy?" White grabbed Ulzana by the hair and repeated his question. The warrior's eyes almost startled the soldier because they were unfathomable. They were not blank yet they were not legible, almost as if the nerves to the brain had been disconnected. Ulzana's face was an impassive mask which was searching White's soul and emotions through indifferent yet sparkling eyes. "Savvy?" Ulzana pointed in the direction they were walking.

"I hear tell you 'paches have supplies hidden away in these mountains. We're gonna need some water soon if I can't find the soldiers. You savvy *water*?" Ulzana looked back at the mountains where so much of him had perished. White grabbed him and almost lifted him bodily. "*Water* you blasted savage! " Ulzana reacted automatically as he kicked at his tormentor but White blocked it as if by instinct then lashed out with a rock-hard fist which made the warrior fall with a thud. "There isn't goin' to be anything left when I get through with you, 'pach. I know you got some waterhole around here some place and you're gonna tell me." White yanked the beads Ulzana was wearing around his neck and flung them in his face. "*Water!* " Next came the turkey-red bandana that was around Ulzana's head. White saw the turquoise earring that dangled through the savage's pierced ear and tore it out of place without a moment's hesitation. "Savvy *water*?" Ulzana didn't utter a sound as he turned his ear toward the sand in order to clot the blood. White broke off a needle from a nearby cactus and tore open Ulzana's dusty shirt. "I'm gonna give you one more chance, 'pache. *Water.* Where is some *water*? " For the first time White almost studied Ulzana's face: the long, straight black hair around a rather large head; a heavy broad nose, a low wrinkled forehead, a full strong chin. The eyes were like two cruel pieces of obsidian with a fire behind them. The mouth seemed to be a sharp, straight, thin lipped gash without one softening feature. White could not have imagined crueller features and he did not hesitate to stab Ulzana's chest with the cactus needle. The deep chest writhed with every penetration of the needle but except for labored breathing there was not a sound. White finally stopped when the dark copper chest was turning red. It was no use, they'd have to be spotted by the cavalry or make it to the fort. "On your feet. Remember, if I die I'm taking you with me." White neglected to pick up his rifle as the two men resumed their march.

At high noon the sun was a raging flood of infinite fire. The sky was a blue lid on an oven of thirst, the landscape became a sea of boiling lava over which Ulzana and White had to swim as the hours paced by. White searched for some signs of life but there was no panting jackrabbit, no lizard, not even a bird to give some hope of life. The soldier stumbled and consequently put his hand to the sand only to find his palm blistered from the scorching sand. He wanted to pause and rest but there was no shade, just billows of heat, so he continued to follow the Indian until the sun set. It seemed a bit cooler with the terrific glare gone. A faint breeze faltered now and then as White reclined against a rock. While the air was something like the breath of a furnace it was a welcome change from the stagnant heat of the day. Ulzana's large black eyes looked only toward the mountains he had abandoned while the soldier tried to gather his senses to look for water and food. When he spied the towers of the giant sahuaro life streamed back into his body. Sahuaro! Wasn't there water in them?! Down at the bottom! He pushed his Indian captive toward the desert candelabra and when the men got to the first one White began to stab at it with his knife. Ulzana's unfathomable sparkling eyes merely watched the white man as he picked and poked at the desert plant in his frenzied efforts to wrench water from it. White put some of the pulp in his mouth but there was scant moisture in it. It was a lie, a cheat: there was no water in it ... it was barren as the sand, thirsty as the sun, cruel as nature itself.

As the moon was coming up White saw a lizard scurrying from one bush to another. Without a moment's hesitation the soldier threw himself on the little creature, captured it, ate what he could of it. He saw another lizard but was unable to grab it. *"I'll get something to eat during the night. Gotta tie the 'pache ... damn his blood ...blood."* The Apache was made of flesh and blood ... and it was a question of survival. White cocked his pistol and pointed it at the Indian's temple.

The moon danced on Ulzana's dark features. He looked at the gun barrel then back at the soldier. For the first time he smiled, revealing his ultra-white teeth which somehow reminded the white soldier of a lion or tiger. *"Wa-ti-hes ti-kot-ito,"* remarked Ulzana, speaking for the first time since his capture in a voice with qualities which White couldn't describe. White was so taken aback that he almost regained his composure, momentarily forgetting his cannibalistic thirst and hunger.

"What?! " was all the soldier said. Then he bared his teeth and slugged the Indian across the face. This time it was a knockout blow for Ulzana did not move as White bound his captive's feet with his soldier's belt. Certain that the Apache could not escape, the soldier walked about in an effort to find some nourishment, a hollow rock full of rain water, an oasis. All that seemed to exist was the giant shadow of the sahuaro: empty, lifeless, cruel ... but somehow beckoning, hopeful. White encountered only illusion in the sahuaro jungle. After what seemed hours of hunting the shadows of the sahuaros began to lean this way and that, tilting, dancing a weird, menacing ritual. *"Wa-ti-hes ti-kot-iti."* White froze.

"Who said that? Where are you? " he said aloud.

"WA-TI-HES TI-KOT-IT."

Something moved and the soldier fired at it. He heard a noise behind him and fired more shots through the silvery moonlight. He stumbled into a cactus bush, the searing pain of the needles entering his flesh gave him another shock which wasn't illusion. Suddenly he realized he shouldn't waste time resting. He had to travel at night, right now! Bone-weary or not it was his only chance to survive. He retraced his trail to the Apache, pulled him to his feet and shouted, "Fort Huachuca! "

Ulzana's moon-lit face showed only its strong, impassive features. There was no gesture, no smile, no twitch to demonstrate he had heard the shots from the pistol. White didn't realize the warrior was probing his faint gasping for breath, the meaning of the shots in the night, even the delicate traces of where the cactus needles penetrated. Ulzana was aware of the white soldier's situation. He missed no sound, no clue, no trace. All were noted. All were understood. He continued to lead the way through the moonlight as White followed behind him. Thirst and hunger had long ago begun to gnaw away at his being and he knew he would have to have something to eat and drink soon. He kept himself going mile after mile by concentrating on yellow hair and black hair. Yellow. Black. Hair. His hands would have to be freed if he was going to save himself. The mountains. Hair.

Just before dawn Ulzana heard the white soldier yelling something. He stopped his walk and turned to see his enemy sprawled on the sand, pistol in hand. Two bullets sped by him and then the death knell of a *click!* made the firearm useless. White let it fall to the ground, stumbled to his feet, took out his knife. "You go too, 'pache," he said as he cut the leather strips that had imprisoned Ulzana's hands behind his back since the beginning of the journey. The handcuffs were still in place, however, so White knocked down the Indian, sat on him, unlocked the brown left wrist and put the cuff on his own wrist. He hurled the key as far as he could and said, "If I die so will you." His speech was difficult because his tongue was so swollen. "Now git," he ordered as he flung his knife away.

The blistering heat returned with the sun and soon White was walking less and being pulled more by the brown wrist. Soon he began to stumble but he managed to pull himself back to his feet each time, saying, "You'll die too, 'pache." His eyes became more and more dazed, his large muscles began to respond less and less until when the sun was directly overhead he stumbled to the smoldering sand and didn't get up.

Ulzana dragged his enemy for a hundred yards or so before he turned to look at the yellow hair. No, he wasn't dead yet, not quite. But it was only a question of a few more hours in the land where the Apache warrior was disputed but king. Ulzana pulled out a hunting knife from his knee-high war moccasin. It had been concealed in the heavy buckskin all the time, ready for use when needed. Ulzana's first thought was to hack away at the soldier's sunburned wrist but then the thought of his family in the cave flashed through his mind. The white man's fort was not too far away . . . he would have to take another chance. He returned to his march and looked for something to eat until he saw a large greasewood bush with a dry tangle of leaves and twigs all around it. With his knife he dug at the roots of the bush and discovered a litter of fat prairie mice. He feasted on the dozen or so that he caught and then spied a rattlesnake resting in a neighboring bush. Ulzana stood and whipped White's semi-lifeless body into the coiled rattler, thus inviting the snake to sink its venom in the white soldier. Before the rattler could recoil Ulzana picked it up from the tail and broke its neck with two quick whiplashes. Once the skin was off the delicate gray meat became a tasty meal indeed. The warrior saw the mescal plant but had no time to make use of its life-giving qualities. He resumed his march toward the white man's war village, not even bothering to look back at the carcass he was dragging, his brown hands grasping the soldier's wrist. White's dead body made a furrow in the sand and the corpse was almost the color of the burning ocean in which it was being dragged.

Ulzana's thoughts wandered from his early life back to the cave, from the Apache way of life to the cave, from the yellow-haired homesteaders to the cave . . . always the cave, the cave. An ocean could not have drowned out his loss, his anguish, his love, his hate. It was the second family he had lost to the white soldiers who delighted in the massacre of Apaches. He had felt death both times . . . the cave . . . the burning lodge filled with odor of burning flesh . . . the white soldiers and the yellow hair . . . the children crying for help from their warrior father . . . hair . . . HAIR . . . Ulzana stood motionless. He had heard hoofbeats. They were still in the distance but he was sure of it . . . yes, over there, ponies of the white soldiers . . . about a dozen. Ulzana grinned the smile of death as he looked back at White. He would kill another white soldier just as certainly as he had planned to kill the one he had held prisoner since the two enemies had begun their march. The Apache warrior went down on one knee and threw dirt all over himself then he staggered this way and that in the direction of the soldiers for he was certain the enemy would soon be watching him through their magic eyes which made things come close when they were far. Ulzana seemed to faint from exhaustion at just the precise moment and within a few minutes the soldiers rode up and encircled him and the corpse.

"Detail . . . halt! " ordered the soldier in command. "Careful with that Apache, I think he's still kicking."

"He's half dead," said another soldier as all dismounted, with the exception of the sergeant, looking at the Indian then inspecting the soldier's body. "Dead," finished the soldier.

"Shoot the chain off the cuffs and we'll drag the Apache back to the fort," ordered the white leader.

A rifle shot freed the living from the dead.

"Lift the renegade up and I'll put this rope around his neck," said the soldier as he bent out of his saddle. "You two put the dead man on a horse so we can give him a Christian —"

Ulzana had come to life and plunged his knife deep into the heart of the white soldier, pulling him out of the saddle and propelling himself into it almost before the other soldiers realized. The horse was off in a thundering gallop as a soldier bellowed, "He got the sergeant! Get 'im! After 'im! "

Ulzana spurred his horse toward his mountain refuge as bullets whizzed by him on all sides. He handled the horse as if it had been his own personal mount but he was conscious only of some homesteaders he knew, homesteaders with yellow hair. The horse's thundering hoofbeats took him further from and closer to his eternal enemies. *If he could just make it to the mountains . . .*

II

ACCULTURATION

"Anda hijito, levántate."

"Morning, Dad. What time is it? "

"Six-fifteen. Come on, up and at 'em. Those defensive ends are waiting to stick you."

The father and the son went into their respective bathrooms then returned to their bedrooms to dress for the morning run. They pulled on their sweat suits, sweat socks, then their bright yellow running shoes with the built-in arch supports.

"¿Ya estás? " asked the father.

"Yes," replied the son as he put on a blue beanie. "Got the ball? "

The father slapped the football loudly. It felt slippery. But footballs had always felt slippery to him.

The pair left the house and were on the dirt road in seconds. They did a few stretching movements to limber up then broke into a slow trot, still warming up. The ball was pitched back and forth until the two came to the road which led to the highway. Then it was passed from one to the other but it wasn't until the highway was crossed that the ball was thrown with zinging force. The runners were now thoroughly warmed up and they ran at half speed, passing the football back and forth.

"Concentrate! " yelled the father as the son missed a pass. "It's all concentration — you have good hands — concentrate on that ball." The father was breathing harder now but he noticed his son's cold blue eyes focus on the ball from the time it was raised to the split second it arrived into his hands The father purposely threw the pigskin just a little off every once in a while to develop his son's reactions.

"This is far enough, Dad," said the son as they came to the bend in the road where they usually turned back to return home.

"Okay, come on, let's go."

HEARTLAND

"Rest a minute, I'm tired."

"Come on, All State, I'm not winded."

"Maybe you're in better condition than I am," said the son.

"*Ya mero.*"

"Coach gave me a compliment yesterday."

"What? "

"He said I was the toughest tight end in the state."

"Really? " said the father.

"Yeah."

"He ought to see you gasping now. Come on."

They started running again, the father throwing a hard pass at his son. In the entire run of about a mile the football would be thrown and caught from fifty to a hundred times. They would stop running a block from their house in order to cool off.

"Look at the sun behind the mountain," remarked the son as the two walked toward the house, both runners breathing heavily but now beginning to feel the elation of a completed morning run.

"Peaceful," said the father.

Once back inside the home the father went to shave while the son made breakfast. He peeled potatoes, sliced them, put them into the skillet where he already had the cooking oil hot. They sizzled menacingly but he covered the skillet quickly and went to the refrigerator where he got out the steak, cut off two pieces on the cutting board, then floured and put them in another skillet to cook slowly.

The father came into the kitchen to put on the herb tea. He wasn't finished dressing yet so he returned to his bedroom. When he emerged again the tea was ready so he shut off the electric burner.

"You wanna fry the eggs, Dad? "

"Yes."

Four eggs were fried quickly and the man served all the food on two large plates. The son got the vitamin bottles out of the fridge and began separating the various capsules.

"How many alfalfas you want? "

"Two. You take two C's if that cold is still trying to catch you." The father put the heaping plates on the table then poured the tea through a strainer, squeezed some lemon into the steaming liquid, and sweetened it with honey while the son poured orange juice for himself. They sat down together and said grace.

"Go ahead," said the father as he bowed his head.

"*En el nombre del Padre, el Hijo, el Espíritu Santo,*" intoned the son as both made the sign of the cross. "*Gracias a Dios que nos dio de comer, sin merecerlo, a la Divina Providencia que nos dio casa, vestido, sustento.*"

"For love and strength and daily bread we praise thy name, O Lord," said the father.

"Amen," they chanted together.

"Why did he say you were the toughest tight end in the state? " asked the father as the two began eating.

"I dunno."

"A *penco** like you."

"Why do you say that? "

"*Anda,* don't be so world serious. You're only seventeen, too young to be an old fool. Did you salt the potatoes? "

"Yeah."

"*Yes.*"

"Yes."

"Don't say *yeah.*"

"Maybe he was just trying to make up for the other day," reflected the son.

"Coach? "

"Yeah. *Yes.*"

"What happened? "

"This guy was bullying a couple of the smaller guys, sophomores. So when it was my turn I gave him a shot. Knocked him over and he rolled a couple of times. Coach said if I ever did that again in practice he would take me on himself."

"What did you say? "

"Just 'Yes, sir.' I guess he hadn't seen why I did it."

"Good. Did you talk to somebody new yesterday? "

"No, not really."

"Have you been talking to the Mexican girls? "

"I can't just walk up to them."

"*¿Por qué no?* "

"What if they don't want to talk to me? "

"Oh come on. Everybody goes for the football gladiators. They're so big and dumb and — "

"Ah Dad."

"Of course they want to talk to you. Why, they want to go out with you. There you are with that big Spanish name, that black hair, green-blue eyes —"

"Green blue? "

"The left one is green this morning. But you have to try to get to know them, especially the quiet ones. What do you think it does to them if they see you just with gringas? "

"I don't pick my friends that way."

"Well, I don't either, but remember everybody sees who you *peeck.*"

"Ah Dad."

"What? "

"You're obsolete."

"Pero mira que pícaro. Do you miss your Spanish class this year?

"Well, I . . . if . . . no, not really."

*a motherless calf.

HEARTLAND

"After five years of Spanish the school system doesn't have a course for your senior year. Man, public education. What class do you like best? "

"I dunno. Shop maybe. The teacher jokes around but he's real strict so nobody will get hurt."

"Good. What other classes? "

"Speech is fun too. I like them all, really. You know, Dad —"

"Sure, I know him. He's a great guy."

"I'm sort of getting tired of steak every morning," said the son, ignoring his father's remark.

"You don't like beans, you're tired of meat, what do you think I should feed you? "

"I like beans. That chile is just too hot. I ate a dozen corn tortillas yesterday. Why don't we make some in the morning? "

"We can't have them for breakfast too. Wait till wrestling season rolls around, you'll be dying to eat anything. You've got to eat heavy if you're going to compete in football. A hundred and seventy pounds is light for a tight end."

"Okay."

"Everybody got mad at me at my university class yesterday," said the father.

"Oh, why? "

"They were carrying on about the Aztecs. Some Chicanos like to make the Aztecs out to be the greatest. So I told them I didn't understand why, since they were little more than militaristic cannibals. Everybody said, 'agh, crap! ' So I told 'em there was lots of documentation in the library. No takers, though." The father sipped on his tea.

"They were cannibals? "

"Sure were. They averaged about one hundred thousand human sacrifices a year and they made *tamales* out of human flesh."

"Really? " exclaimed the son.

"Now the Mayas were a great people. Very advanced. So were the Incas. But the Aztecs were anything but enlightened. They could fight and had enough sense to borrow from other cultures, that's all."

"Did they believe you? "

"I don't know. I'm a lot older than most of the people in there, but I don't know if that makes any difference to them anymore. It doesn't really matter. I'm just tired of hearing how 'cruel and greedy' the Spaniards were and how great the Aztecs were. Heck, everybody that's come to this country has come to make money. I said that to the class and one gal, a black kid, said, 'Oh yeah? ' So I pointed out that I had used the word *come,* not *brought.*"

"What did she say? "

"Everybody laughed. I hope she didn't get mad. I didn't mean it as a put down, but blacks didn't *come* here, they were forced."

"In my Minorities class we studied that a lot of whites were indentured so they were brought too. But why are they putting down the Spanish in Chicano Studies? "

"They think they have to do that to show pride in the Indian side of our heritage. But I believe it's because they've been acculturated by books that have portrayed the Spanish as villains so Hispanics won't know how much their people have accomplished. If our heroes are made into bad guys then we aren't worth much ourselves."

"What do you mean? "

"Well, some people don't like to admit the Spanish did things like discovering America. The Vikings did it or an Italian did it, anybody but the Spanish and Catholic Spain. It's okay if our people are janitors. 'Hewers of wood and drawers of water,' somebody once wrote in a national magazine. But they would never think of us as descendants of world discoverers."

"But we are."

"Yes, and someday even school books will admit it," said the father.

"Come to think of it, all the janitors and cooks at school are Chicanos."

"Say, did you hear that a group of Chicano writers are putting together the Chicano version of *Roots?* "

"Great! Even I will buy a copy. What are they going to call it? " asked the son.

"*Grass.* "

"Ah Dad! "

"*Chihuahua!* Look at the time. Gotta rush! Anybody ever tell you that you talk too much at breakfast, *penco*? " The father picked up the dishes and put them in the sink. He went into his bedroom and came out shortly, ready to go to work. "Okay, make sure you close all the windows before you leave. Study hard and have a good practice." He walked over to his son and put his arm around him, turning his head slightly. The son kissed his father's cheek. "I'll see you tonight. We don't need anything from the store? "

"I don't think so."

"*Bueno.* I'll see you. And don't forget to talk to those Mexican girls, especially the little quiet ones," he said as he hurried toward the door. "Don't forget your lunch money. What's the cafeteria serving today? "

The son opened the cabinet where the school lunch menu for the month was thumb-tacked. "Oh-oh," he said.

"What is it? "

"*Tamales.* "

III

MISTRESS OF THE PLAINS

The stragglers munched on the rich prairie grass but the sentinels lifted their heads and appeared to nod into the wind as they sniffed. There was no mistaking the scent: men. The sentinels snorted their alarm to the stragglers and immediately all the horses dashed to the main body of the herd. The stallion commanders of each band in the herd took charge to make the horses respond with the precision and regularity of a well-trained cavalry unit. Each band maintained its wheeling distance from the other bands but there were so many horses running the whole country seemed to be on the move. From a distance the entire prairie near the horizon appeared to be moving with long undulations like waves of the ocean.

Three mustangers, all yelling and waving blankets, had caused the avalanche of wild animals to sweep away like a strikingly beautiful tornado of abandoned freedom. The herd ran for about three miles, coursing with the speed of the wind, the horses tossing their proud necks and flowing manes into the air, leaping and curvetting in the distance, seeming to delight in the cloud of dust they raised.

Waiting behind a little hill was a fourth mustanger, a fourteen year old girl named Valeria Márquez who was a unique veteran at capturing wild horses. She waited as the herd approached her hiding place, then as the animals began passing, the light of the sun shimmering off their streaking bodies, the thunder of their hooves like a roar of the surf on a rocky coast, Valeria spurred her mount, Nuflo, and suddenly she was a part of the racing prairie. She fixed her attention on a chestnut that came up alongside her and as Nuflo became aware this was the horse they wanted he moved closer, ever closer, making the chestnut separate from the rest of the thundering herd. Valeria could tell the mustang was nearly winded but the horse still ran smoothly as it separated from the main herd. Valeria now made Nuflo almost touch the mustang and carefully measured the space between her and the wild horse. Nuflo was now striding exactly with the mustang. Valeria had the ten-foot hair rope looped around her right shoulder and as Nuflo put her within striking distance of the mustang's back she raised her right arm to grab the wild mane. Suddenly she was a foot too far away so she poked her left knee into Nuflo's side.

The mustang was aware that something was happening but instinct had led him to rely on speed in the first place and now he resorted anew to his basic wisdom of running like the wind. But the beautiful wild horse was tiring fast, its strength failing quicker than that of the gelding on its side for Nuflo had not run nearly as much this afternoon.

Valeria again raised her right hand and this time was able to grab the mustang's mane. With her left hand she grasped the mane of her own horse, put her left knee on the sheepskin that served as her saddle, and pushed herself onto the mustang's back. She felt the usual elation of changing horses and not falling but her mind turned instantly to looping the hair rope over the mustang's head. She accomplished this on her first effort. Now came the more difficult maneuver of throwing a half hitch upward around the mustang's nose. The animal was slowing down but a fall at this speed could still be deadly so she grabbed the mane tightly with her left hand and swung the rope in the manner to produce the half-hitch and send it up around the nose. She missed the first three times but she got it on the fourth. The wild horse became confused and tried to run faster but the rope clung vigorously to its muzzle, thus preventing free movement of the head. Valeria was able to put another half-hitch into place and now she let him run, guiding him in the general direction of the camp by pulling on the hair rope.

The mustang ran for a couple of miles more, then he was thoroughly winded. The wild horse was aware that some creature was on its back, that its muzzle was in some kind of powerful grip, but there was no pain involved and his running instinct was a prisoner of complete exhaustion so he merely walked in whatever direction it was easiest to take.

Valeria was in complete control of the mustang. She looked around for Nuflo but he didn't appear immediately, though she knew he'd come momentarily to help lead the captured prize. She turned around slightly and saw three riders in the distance. That would be her father, mother, and older brother. The mustang continued to move, walking mostly, but trying to catch its wind and run again. Nuflo showed up and came up alongside the mustang, somewhat calming the wild horse.

Valeria's family caught up with her and the men immediately threw ropes on the mustang. The girl jumped off the chestnut and mounted Nuflo.

"What a glorious prize! " said the mother, María Magdalena.

"What a good little prize that daughter of mine is! " said the father, Emilio Márquez, as he leaned over toward Nuflo and put his hand gently behind Valeria's neck for the briefest moment. "Let's go back to camp. The herd has gone too far to follow today. We can do some breaking."

"Maybe Valeria would like to do that too? " teased Fernando, the family's bronco buster. He used to capture horses the way Valeria now did until he got too heavy, thus losing the agility that was so important to accomplish the feat.

Indeed, the mother and father had captured horses the way the children did, Emilio having broken both arms and legs over the years. But the exciting art had not died out when they got older for they had taught it to their children.

"No," returned Valeria, "that's the part I can't stand and you well know it."

"*Anda,* you just don't want to do the hard part," continued Fernando, smiling broadly all the while.

"Don't be such a tease, Fernando," said María Magdalena.

"Come on, *mamacita,*" replied Fernando, the big smile never leaving his face, "Valeria knows how to laugh."

"Who wouldn't, with you around," said Valeria.

"Let's get back to camp," said Emilio Márquez to his family. "America and Luisa will be waiting to see what we caught."

Emilio and María Magdalena enjoyed a measure of regional fame in their section of the plains. They had been mustangers all their lives and they had little difficulty selling all the horses they could catch. Mustangs captured by the Márquez clan had never been abused by pursuing them until they were so tired they were ruined for life. They were never captured by stationary snares that came close to choking the horse to death. And never was mustang shot or creased on the spine to stun it long enough to get a rope on it. In all their years of mustanging Emilio and Magdalena had never seen anyone marksman enough to capture a mustang with a rifle. The bullet either missed altogether or killed the horse by shattering its spine.

Emilio had an easy command of horses, a special understanding of them, and together with his wife they had passed on their profession to their children. Together they had known toil and hardship, sometimes hunger and thirst. But they felt the beat of a hardy lifestyle in their veins, and theirs was the glory of work and the joy of living. They knew their profession was potentially violent but it also had its unparalleled independence, beauty, and nobility. For example, last year the family had managed to capture a beautiful stallion commander. When the fiery animal was finally subdued he merely stood. The whole family was concerned but Valeria especially tried to make him eat and drink the nourishment which she took him every day. The stallion would have none of it. He would rather die than lose his freedom. On the sixth day of the mustang's hunger strike Emilio and Magdalena knew what had to be done. By the tenth day the horse would be dead, so they told the children to set the horse free.

Valeria was the first to walk up to the magnificent animal and untie him. Fernando ran the palm of his hand across the mustang's back, a powerful back he would never ride. Luisa and America merely patted the animal's side in farewell. The horse had to be pushed to make him start walking Once he started he didn't stop but he never increased his speed while he was within eyesight of the family. Neither did he look back. There was *animal* as well as *human* nobility on the Great Plains.

The Márquez camp was shaded by brush and close to water. Emilio and Fernando hunted wild meat whenever it was necessary and Magdalena baked bread and cooked in a round *horno* beehive oven. The family necessities were moved in a large *carreta* which had two high wheels and was drawn by three big burros. The corral had been built against a rock bluff, three sides of it made of limbs and brush packed down between pairs of well planted posts, about two feet apart, that were lashed together at the top with rawhide.

America and Luisa rushed out to meet their family and inspect the new prize. The girls were only nine and eight years old but their mustang traditions enabled them to appreciate the high tossing head, dilated nostrils, sleek hair, prominent eye, tapered nose, rounded breast, slender legs, small hooves.

"Well, what do my daughters think? " asked Emilio. America and Luisa smiled, their eyes shining a hearty approval. Their ambition in life was to capture horses the way their sister did. Until then they had to be content with herding the animals Valeria caught.

"*Papi*, she is strong," said Luisa to her father.

"Yes, *hijita*, now let's put her with the others."

The mare was led to the corral where there were more than a dozen other horses. None had been broken to the saddle yet but the process might as well begin immediately, so Fernando brought out his equipment while Magdalena went to prepare for the afternoon meal. Perhaps she was too much like Valeria. She didn't enjoy this part of her profession, though it was necessary and not evil. Maybe she would cook something special tonight . . .

Emilio and Fernando cut out a sorrel mare from the herd. Fernando threw his rawhide lariat around the horse's neck then quickly anchored the rope to his saddle horn. He dismounted and prepared to put a blinder on the mustang, which was rearing up fiercely, screaming resistance and pawing the air mightily. The long mane and tail floated out in the air, almost like liquid gold, as the sun and activity made the animal sweat.

Emilio and Valeria took their lariats and each roped one of the horse's front ankles. Now when the animal reared, fire and destruction in its eye, her forelegs were pulled out from under her, causing her to land on her knees or even lose her balance and fall to her side. The horse struggled back to her feet after every fall, but each time she reared it taught her a quick lesson.

When the mustang quieted down Fernando walked up, cautiously but confidently, talking to the animal in a quiet voice. He patted the neck and ran his hand down the length of it. He brought the blindfold into position and was able to secure it on the second try. He allowed the horse to become accustomed to the blindfold, then he set about running his hands over the animal's back. Next he put the saddle pad on the horse, and finally, without too much difficulty, the saddle.

The mustang started bucking but the forefeet were pulled out immediately and the sorrel crashed to the ground. She was quiet after that so Fernando removed the blindfold. With the return of sight the mustang reared up again only to wind up on her knees.

"Ready to mount," said Fernando as he approached the horse and grabbed the saddle horn with his left hand.

Emilio thought it was a bit too soon but all he said was, "Get ready,

Valeria."

Fernando bounded into the saddle and the sorrel seemed to acquire a belly full of bedsprings, pawing at the sun, breaking in two halfway up, sunfishing on the way down, then hitting the earth hard enough to crack open Fernando's liver. Valeria thought she had been ready but the rope nearly slipped out of her hand with the sudden jolt. She grabbed it tightly at the last instant and with her father, the horse was brought to her knees. But the sorrel would not be licked so easily. She rolled over, trying to crush the rider underneath her bulk. Fernando went sprawling to avoid the horse's murderous weight but he was agile and quick enough to spring back into the saddle by the time the sorrel began to get back on her feet. It was as if the rider had never been off.

Valeria grasped the rope and gritted her teeth, determined not to be surprised again. But the fight seemed to have gone out of the sorrel for she stood trembling with fear, bruised from the falls, made submissive by the imprisoning ropes. Valeria was overcome with a deep pity, a wounding sympathy. A mustang had to be free to be a mustang and freedom was motion, running, dashing across a level or over a rise, wild and free.

"Good, good," said Emilio, "she will make an excellent mount. Let's lace her up."

Fernando dismounted quickly and when the horse reared a few feet she was brought down to the ground. A rope was tied around a fetlock joint, the other end around the lower neck, thus bringing the animal under control by forcing her to hop wherever she wanted to go.

"Look, look! " yelled Magdalena. "The stallion! " Everyone turned. Not two hundred yards away the stallion commander was voicing his challenge as he pawed the air. The fiery leader of the herd had come to free his mares. The flaming cascade of his mane, the curving comet of his tail, flag of his noble heritage, caused the mares to believe their leader had come to their rescue. At first the entire Márquez family looked in admiration at the magnificent stallion. He came closer, charging at the camp with his iron muscles rippling all over him, the refined head set with determination, bones that must have had the density of ivory, pounding steel hooves, the flames of vitality burning in every fiber of his body and spirit.

"We've got to stop him or he'll stampede the mares," said Emilio. "Magdalena, *querida*, guard the children and the camp." The father knew that a mustang stallion was the most vicious animal on four legs. Emilio, Valeria, and Fernando sprang to their horses as the stallion veered to his right, barely missing the heart of the camp. The three mustangers lit out in pursuit, chasing him for more than a mile only to see the splendid stallion outdistance them as easily as if they had been running races with the wind. The stallion disappeared behind a rise but Valeria, riding to the left of her father and brother, suddenly came upon a half dozen horses that bolted away as she approached. Out of instinct, Nuflo, a bit tired but too well trained not to take advantage of the good luck, raced toward the closest animal and put Valeria within striking distance of the wild mustang's back.

Valeria quickly put the horsehair rope on her shoulder for she was as

HEARTLAND

willing as her horse. She put her arm out to grab the wild one's mane and grasped it firmly. As she put her knee in position to change horses she suddenly thought of the trembling, fear-ridden mustang that was being broken to the saddle and captivity. This caused her to hesitate for an instant and the mustang bolted forward as she leaped toward the wild horse. Valeria grabbed the wild mane with both hands as her feet hit the ground and dragged on the rich grass. She tried desperately to hook her right leg over the mustang's back but somehow the horse veered away sufficiently to prevent it. Valeria lifted her legs up so that a hoof would not hit them but as she hung on her arms were becoming weary and her grip on the mane was becoming weaker, slipping slowly. The horse continued to race like a tornado as an eternity passed for Valeria. She prepared to let go, trying to pick a spot to fall but the earth was speeding by much too fast. She made one last effort to throw her leg over the animal's back but she was much too tired and gravity finally brought her to earth, arms and legs pressed up tightly to her chest, but head over heels, rolling over and over. A dull pain took control of the world.

Valeria was unaware of hoofbeats retreating into the distance nor of those approaching as fast as possible. She was unaware of anything except a slow-moving, inky domain with occasional spots of light. Darkness struggled with flashes of light until darkness conquered all.

When Valeria began to regain consciousness she saw two misty shapes bending over her. The figures gradually solidified into her father and brother.

"Where do you hurt, *hijita*? " asked Emilio.

"*Papi*? " moaned Valeria.

"Yes, precious girl, I'm right here." He ran his hands gently over her neck, shoulders, arms, her entire body. Nothing seemed to be broken but . . .

Valeria sat up slowly.

"You all right, Sis? " asked Fernando as he sat beside her and gently put a hand on her back to see if anything had happened to her spine.

"I – I think so." She rolled her neck slowly from side to side.

"Where does it hurt? " asked her father.

"E–everywhere, but I don't think anything is broken."

"Can you stand? " asked Fernando.

"No, not yet," cautioned the father, "just sit there. Fernando, return to camp to make sure the stallion didn't circle back. Valeria and I will follow in a little while."

Fernando was no sooner out of sight when Valeria burst into tears.

"No, my little girl, don't cry. Tell me where it hurts."

"In my heart," sobbed Valeria uncontrollably. "I can't do it anymore."

Emilio was taken aback by the sudden gush of tears. He felt his daughter was not seriously hurt physically, just bruised, but something else was very wrong. "What can't you do anymore, *hijita*? "

"The mustangs are so wild and free," sobbed the girl, "then we take away their beauty, their *freedom*."

"Oh my little love."

"I can't do it anymore," sobbed Valeria. "I fell in the middle of my jump."

"You have fallen before and I fell many times."

"That's not it, *Papi*," explained the girl as she began to get a hold of herself. "As I was leaving Nuflo for the mustang I thought of how he would soon be trembling with fear, being knocked down by the ropes . . ." Valeria began to sob again, but more quietly. "I can't do it anymore, *Papi,* I can't take away their freedom."

"Yes, I see, my lovely, I see," consoled Emilio. Very gently he put his arms around his daughter and just held her. The thought had crossed his mind that Valeria had almost lost the rope when they breaking the sorrel mare, judging by the strength of the yank on his rope. "Come on, sweet one," said the father, "let's stand up and walk around a while."

Valeria managed to get to her feet and though she had a layer of grass all over her there was no sharp pain. Emilio was immensely relieved. He knew Valeria needed to be talked to, to have things explained. It had been coming, he could see it clearly now.

"You know, my darling, we have been mustangers all our lives," he began. "If I couldn't work with horses I don't think I could go on living. After you, your mother, Fernando, and your sisters, the deepest love I have is for the horses, the wild free ones as well as those that make their lives with us. Look at your Nuflo over there. He would never leave you and you love him for it. He's not a slave, though he works very hard. But then we all work hard.

"I don't know what a prisoner is, *reina mora,* for I have never been one. I am as free as the wild mustangs, and I have given you the same life because it is the best life. We belong on the plains and the mustangs are the most beautiful, the most spirited and inspiring creatures in this extraordinary world that is ours forever." Emilio stopped for a moment and gazed at his daughter. She wasn't crying any longer but she looked faint and pale.

"Here, let's sit here on the grass," said the father. They sat side by side, facing opposite directions, their arms around each other. "Life on the plains has been the best life for me and your mother. I have seen barbed wire in some parts of the country and eventually it will destroy the open range, I guess. I don't like to think about it and I will be gone before it happens but you will always remember the way we lived. Sometimes our life is happy, sometimes it's sad, but we have never been alone. You have people with you, your people who care about you and will never leave you.

"Someday you will meet a man, a mustanger like you. It is a mighty good thing to know men, not from looking at them, but from having been one of them. You will marry him the way your mother and I married, and you will have beautiful children like I do. You will teach them to love the plains, the buffalo, the antelope, the turkeys, the wild plums. But most of all you will teach them to love the horses, the beautiful mustangs, even the hammer-heads, maybe." Valeria hugged her father a little tighter. He wasn't quite sure what it meant but it made him think of when she was a babe in arms. The years had vanished almost without warning.

"I remember when you were a little girl, just learning to ride. We came upon a bunch of horses but they didn't run away. I think they just stood there looking at you, wondering what that was so tiny sitting on a horse. It was springtime and a south wind was blowing over the new grass and flowers. You actually saw one horse looking at you then putting his head down to smell the flowers. He did it several times and you said, '*Papi*, is he smelling the flowers or waiting to eat them?' We all laughed, especially Fernando.

"We capture the beautiful horses because we appreciate beauty, my darling. We cannot live at ease with ugliness so we go after the well-formed mustangs, the courageous ones, so when they share our lives they will enrich it with their beauty and strength. In a way you could say we take away their freedom but is it so bad what we give them in return? Nuflo would never leave us. Nuflo. I still think that's a weird name." Emilio saw a faint smile forming on his daughter's mouth.

"You know we don't abuse the horses, Valeria. Once, when I was still a very young man, I hired on with this gringo outfit. We were after a white stallion and no matter how we tried he always got away. When we were sure we couldn't get him we found him asleep in the brush, as luck would have it. The head boss said, 'Since I can't capture it I'll just shoot it.' The man took out his rifle and murdered that beautiful horse, simply because we couldn't capture it. I drew my pay the next day and went on my way. Any man who is a man can't be indifferent to ugliness.

"But we have to have horses, Valeria, and you know it. What is a man without a horse? A man on foot is no man at all. When I'm working I'm no better than my horse. Neither are you, or your mother, or Fernando. A horse and rider are a team, a blending of flesh, spirit, courage, and intelligence. And love or respect. No, our horses are not slaves, unless people are slaves too. Am I your mother's slave because I love her? Is she mine or yours because she works for us? Are you our slave because you are our mustanger? When you have your husband and you give him beautiful children, is it more slavery? No, my beautiful, never never think that. We all need training and educating. That's all we do to horses when we train them to the saddle. Sometimes it hurts a little to change but if there is love a little bit of hurt is quickly forgotten.

"When you get on your horse and gallop over the prairie or through the brush, when you leap over arroyos or dodge prairie dog holes, when you feel his heart beating against you, you know you are so alive you could lasso an eagle or run races with the wind. You are a mustanger, my beloved, and you are one of the best because you throb with respect for your animals, respect and a lot of love. That's the way it should be. And that's only one of the many reasons why I love you."

Staccato hoofbeats approached from the distance but Emilio and Valeria didn't become aware of them until the horses were a hundred yards away. It was María Magdalena with Luisa and America. Father and daughter stood up as the three horses were reined to a halt.

María Magdalena vaulted off her mount and embraced her daughter. Yes, she was all right; no, she wasn't hurt; yes, she was sure; she and *Papi* had just been talking.

"Well then, shall we go back to camp?" Magdalena looked at her husband.

He nodded at her. Everything was all right. "Come on, supper won't get cooked just by Fernando," said the mother.

Valeria mounted up and America and Luisa directed their horses to each side of Nuflo.

Emilio took Magdalena by the hand and helped her mount. "Are you sure she's all right? " asked the mother.

Emilio got up on his horse and as the couple rode back to camp he explained what had really happened and about their talk. Maria Magdalena understood and suddenly she leaned out of her saddle and kissed her husband on the cheek.

That night Valeria gazed up from her bedding at the limitless sky and twinkling stars. She closed her eyes and saw the billowing plains of grass and the drifts of buffaloes. She heard the howl of the wolves and the star-tingling cries of the little coyotes that intensified the silence of the night. She turned her head slightly and saw the glow of coals from the campfire and a trace of evanescent grayish smoke. Valeria drifted into the realm of sleep where she saw a herd of mustangs standing, eyes shining, nostrils dilated, ears forward. The sea of grass beneath their hooves was green and rich. In the silence and solitude the horses seemed to be moving out of the dawn. They stood high for an instant then dashed away with a flame blended of spirit and nature, wild with life and freedom. But wait. One mare remained behind and Valeria watched her as she gazed far away into the depths of the dawn and gathering day.

IV

UNCLE MIKE

Nicolás enjoyed school and his second grade teacher, Sister Albert, but on a Saturday morning he would wake up at the crack of dawn, pull on his clothes, and walk next door to his grandparent's house where Uncle Mike lived. During the summer Uncle Mike would already be sitting on the bench behind the house, soaking up the early sun as it smiled over the mountains. Lately Nicolás was having to awaken Uncle Mike, who was sleeping later these crisp September mornings.

"Uncle Mike, get up, it's me, Nico," said the boy as he knocked loudly on the back door which opened to Mike's room.

"*¿Eh, qué pasa?*" came from within.

"It's me, Nico. You want to play *tejas?*" asked the boy in Spanish. The door opened after a few minutes. Snow-haired Uncle Mike peeped through the slightly opened door and smiled broadly. He had put on his coveralls but not his shirt and his arms and shoulders looked very heavily muscled to young Nico. "You want to play *tejas?*" asked the boy again as he juggled the large washers in his hand.

Uncle Mike didn't say anything but he saw the washers and nodded. The grin didn't get any smaller, just stayed the same as the door closed. Nico went to the place in the back yard where the holes for the *tejas* had been dug. He cleaned out some sand from inside the holes, which were around seven feet apart, then carefully removed the dirt from around the entrance, taking special precaution not to damage the hard surface. The washers had to be able to slide easily into the hole so the area had to be free of sand, pebbles, and all other obstacles. When the job was finished Nico took a few practice shots, first at one hole then the other. *Tejas* was Nico's favorite game and he had spent many hours practicing over the summer. Indeed, he had become fairly proficient for a boy his age. Last weekend he had even beaten his older brother once, though the brother had tripped him on purpose after the game. Nico had become upset but there was nothing he could do since his brother was older and stronger.

HEARTLAND

Nico had never beaten his brother at marbles but at least he had beaten him once at *tejas.*

Nico was busy aiming and throwing the washers at one hole, going to pick them up, then shooting at the other side when Uncle Mike came out of the house. He hadn't washed his face, Nico noticed, because there was still some sleepy sand around his eyes. Uncle Mike still smiled broadly and his arms swung up and down enthusiastically. He was wearing a hat that was almost too big for his head. "¿Eh? " he said as he walked up to Nico.

"Hi, Uncle Mike, watch this," said the boy as he threw the washer carefully. The metal disc almost went into the hole but not quite. "Doggone it," exclaimed Nico as he prepared to let the other washer fly. He stepped back and carefully took aim, trying to make good his second effort. The washer sailed gracefully through the air but missed. Nico sniffed, shook his head slightly, then walked to shoot from the other side. "Okay, you try it, Uncle Mike."

Uncle Mike pulled something out of his pocket. At first Nico thought it was another washer but then he noticed it was much shinier. The man sailed it through the air and the missile landed a foot beyond the hole in the ground.

"Aw come on Uncle Mike, you can do better than that," said Nico as he went to pick up the miss. It was then he saw it was a brand new silver dollar, shinier and heavier than his washers. "Hey, where'd you get this? ! " asked Nico excitedly. He had never seen Uncle Mike with money before. "Is it yours? "

Mike just grinned and swung his arms up and down.

"Can I shoot it once, just once? " Uncle Mike nodded, or at least Nico thought he did, so he prepared a careful shot. First he rubbed the silver dollar between his two hands, then he felt the ridges all around the coin. He looked at the target and in a graceful swing tossed the dollar straight into the hole. "Wowie! " yelled Nico as he raced to the hole and pulled out the shiny silver. "Did you see that, Uncle Mike? Perfect! " The boy gave the coin to his competitor and said, "Okay, your turn. Betcha can't do it."

Uncle Mike threw the washers, one at a time, then Nico picked them up and returned them to him so he could shoot again. Out of more than two dozen shots, Nico offering instructions each time, Uncle Mike only made one. Nico became exasperated. "You might as well be blinded," said Nico and he pulled Uncle Mike's hat down over his eyes.

The sudden loss of sight caused Uncle Mike to panic. His arms agitated up and down and sideways. He seemed to be struggling to breathe and he moved as if the jaws of a huge animal were around his midsection.

Nico was immediately aware that something was wrong. "Okay, okay, don't . . ." said Nico as he tried to take the hat off but one of Mike's arms caught him on the chest and threw him to the ground. Nico picked himself up and wasn't quite sure what to do when Uncle Mike put both hands to the brim of the hat and jerked it up.

Nico didn't know whether to laugh or cry. Uncle Mike looked so serious. He had struggled so hard against a little old hat! And had Uncle Mike really struck him? He had never been dangerous before but now he wasn't even smiling, his jaw agitating up and down nervously. Uncle Mike's eyes seemed to be watery, as if he was going to cry. Then Nico observed something he had never seen before: Uncle Mike's head was small, too small for the rest of his body, and it was kinda pointed at the top, sorta.

Nico's discovery made him forget about being knocked down. It made him forget that he never should have teased Mike in the first place by pulling his hat down over his eyes. He probably wouldn't have thought of doing it if his older brother hadn't done it to him some days before, though he was not aware of it now. Nico's only reaction was to say, "Uncle Mike," and to feel his own head with his right hand. No, it wasn't pointed, just flat. "I'm sorry, Uncle Mike, I shouldn't have pulled your hat. I was only playing. Nico spoke in English and Mike didn't understand it. *"Perdóname,* Uncle Mike. *Domás estaba jugando,"* he repeated in Spanish.

"No hagas eso," said Uncle Mike. His jaw still working nervously he turned and walked back toward the house, entered his room, and shut the door behind him.

Nico just stood for a minute, not knowing what he should do, then he decided to clean the holes of sand and practice some more. He discovered he still had Uncle Mike's silver dollar so he used it. The shiny coin flew gracefully through the air and went into the target several times. Half and hour went by as the boy continued to practice alone.

"Nico, you want to come have breakfast with us? "

The boy looked up and saw his Auntie Lucy standing at her back door. Their house was next to his grandparent's.

"What are you having? "

"Pancakes."

"Sure! "

"Dust yourself off first."

Nico did the best he could to shake and slap off the loose dirt he had gotten on his overalls then he walked over to his aunt's house. He glanced at Uncle Mike's back room but the door was still tightly shut.

"How long have you been up, *Nicolasito*? " asked Auntie Lucy as she poured some batter on the hot griddle.

"Since the sun," Nico replied simply as he came up to the stove and watched the air bubbles form on the pancakes as they began to cook.

"Playing marbles? "

"No, *tejas.* With Uncle Mike." Suddenly Nico remembered about Uncle Mike. "Auntie . . ." he began uncertainly.

"What? " asked the woman as she continued to pour out batter, turn the hotcakes, test the temperature of the syrup, put on coffee, get milk from the refrigerator, and set a place for Nico.

"Auntie . . . why is Uncle Mike . . . kinda . . ."

The aunt stopped and looked at her nephew. For a moment she didn't know what to say, how honest to be, how much young Nico would understand. Then she continued getting breakfast and said, "Uncle Mike is probably the finest person you'll ever meet in your whole life."

"But . . ."

"Yes, he's different from most people, isn't he," continued Auntie Lucy, "but he's different mostly in good ways."

"How old is he, Auntie? "

"Oh, I'd say he's about sixty or seventy."

"Sixty! Gee, he's old. But he has big muscles. His head is funny, sorta."

"There, eat your pancakes. Here's your milk." The woman then fixed herself a plate. "I'm going to eat before the rest of the tribe gets up." She knew she had to make Nico understand about Uncle Mike but how? "Always be good to Uncle Mike, Nico, because he's next to God." The boy looked puzzled. "Yes, he is special in the eyes of God because he has never done any harm to anyone. He has a place ready for him in Heaven. The rest of us have to work for it but Uncle Mike has already won it."

"How come? " asked Nico.

"Because he is the way he is."

The boy pondered this for a moment. "How did he get that way? "

"A famous writer once said that everyone is the way God made him," said Auntie Lucy. "God made Uncle Mike the way he is and he has always been good and gentle. When I was growing up he was the best babysitter you could ever hope to find. We all lived on the ranch then. If Uncle Mike was taking care of someone nothing could happen to him, even on horseback."

"How come he can't play *tejas* or marbles?" . . . asked Nico.

"When you get older you don't do a lot of things you used to. I'm younger than Uncle Mike and I don't play marbles either, though I used to love to."

"Why does he chew so hard when he's not even eating? " asked Nico as he continued his breakfast.

"Don't talk with food in your mouth, *hijito*. I'm sure there's an explanation but I don't know it. I love Uncle Mike, just like you do. God made him that way and he made you the way you are and me the way I am. It's good that we are a family and can love each other even if we're not exactly alike."

"You know why I like Uncle Mike? " asked Nico.

"No, why? "

"Because he always has time to play and I can win him."

"Well, you have to be careful that he doesn't get too tired. He can't do all the things that you do."

Nico reflected a while then said, "I always beat him at *tejas* or marbles but he really doesn't try very hard, even when I give him another chance."

"Uncle Mike is like a saint and we can all learn from him if we want to," said Auntie Lucy. "I'm going to fix his breakfast tray. You want to take it to him? "

"Sure," replied Nico. *Like a saint,* thought the boy. He wondered if all saints had white hair and pointed heads. He felt his own head and wondered if its flatness and black hair would keep him away from sainthood. But maybe there was hope: the only other saints he had ever seen were the statues in the church and none of them looked like Uncle Mike.

"Here," said Auntie Lucy when the tray was ready. "take this to Uncle Mike. Be careful with the coffee. It's very hot, don't spill it on yourself."

Nico took the tray and walked carefully out the door and across the yard, the tray grasped firmly in both hands. His shoulders were bent slightly in a hunched-over effort at protection as he walked. When he got to Uncle Mike's door he laid the tray on the outside bench and knocked.

"Uncle Mike, it's me."

"Eh? " came from within, then the door opened.

"*¿Estás listo pa' comer?* " asked Nico.

Uncle Mike smiled broadly. He was still wearing his hat. Nico picked up the tray, took it inside and laid it on Mike's table. The man sat down, smiled at Nico, and began to eat his pancakes and drink the steaming coffee. Nico sat down on the bed and looked at Uncle Mike, hard, then he thought of the statues in church. There was St. Michael and St. . . . saint . . . the one with all the animals and birds. Ah well, he had a round head anyway, and baldy in the middle. What was it with the heads of all these saints anyway? Maybe he could be a priest if they didn't mind his flat head and black hair.

Uncle Mike ate heartily, and noisily, thought Nico, especially when he slurped his coffee. The boy then reached into his pocket and pulled out Mike's silver dollar. Nico placed it carefully on the tray and Uncle Mike smiled as he took it and put the coin in his own pocket.

The boy put his arm around Uncle Mike and said, "You mustn't eat with your hat on." Gently he took the hat off the man's head and hung it on the coat rack in the corner. Uncle Mike watched the hat carefully as it left his head and journeyed to the rack. When he saw that it was safe he continued his breakfast.

"You like coffee? " asked Nico.

Uncle Mike seemed to nod.

"My daddy makes it every morning and I'm going to bring you a cup." The man smiled. Nico's eyes suddenly lit up. "St. Francis! St. Francis is the one with the baldy head! Do you know him, Uncle Mike? "

CIBOLERO

The two shaggy monsters circle each other cautiously, waiting for the slightest opening to attack. Their great heads, matted with bull nettles and sandburrs, undulate menacingly, alternately raised high then lowered instantly until the huge nostrils almost touch the hard, dry sod. The beasts begin to paw the earth with their hooves, raising clouds of impalpable dust. Then it happens: the buffalo bulls raise their tufted, swollen tails, curve their backs and charge into each other. The thunderous crash is not much cause for concern among the other buffalo who watch disinterestedly as they munch on the prairie grass. One bull raises the whole front portion of his adversary completely off the ground but then falls under the weight. Instantly the bull on top pins his antagonist to the earth, raking him with short, cruel horns. The fallen bull squirms and manages to regain his footing but the fight is over: he moves backward slowly, eyeing the winner while he retreats far enough to scamper away without danger of renewed attack. The victorious bull paws the earth and his eyes send forth livid rays to any who would dare challenge his mastery of the herd.

Downwind from the bison herd and partly hidden in a grove of trees are Rosendo Robles and six other *cazadores,* hunters. They had watched the fight but now they bowed their uncovered heads in silent prayer, beseeching the Lord for a good hunt. They make the sign of the cross, put their hats back on, and ready their lances for the rush at the *cíbolos.* Their prized hunting horses are as ready as they are and begin to prance in expectation and excitement.

"¡*Santiago!* " yells Rosendo Robles and the hunters make a dash for the herd, fanning out in a precision maneuver to assure contact with as many buffalo as possible. The breeze becomes a wind as staccato hoofbeats propel the *ciboleros* and their gleaming, razor sharp lances toward the kings of the plains. The lead cow becomes aware of danger and with a loud bellow stampedes the rest of the herd. The race is on!

Rosendo has the fleetest mount in Alazan so he is the first to make contact with a fleeing beast, his tail high in the air, powerful muscles working to make good the flight from danger. Rosendo takes his lance in both hands and guides Alazan strictly from pressure by his knees. He prepares to thrust with his lance but the buffalo's gait doesn't permit Rosendo to strike immediately. Alazan's gallop begins to duplicate the gait of the buffalo and Rosendo touches the lance to the spot on the ribs where he will thrust before he is ready for the kill. He tightens his knees to Alazan and jams the lance inside the ribs, directly into the heart of the buffalo. The animal's speed causes him to take a few more strides but suddenly he falls head over hooves into a heap. The buffalo is dead before he stops rolling, a perfect kill, and Rosendo prepares for another thrust into another animal.

The hunter suddenly becomes the hunted as a buffalo lunges at Alazan. The horse side-steps the attack as Rosendo sways slightly on the pad which he uses for a saddle. Had it not been for Alazan's training both horse and rider would have been shredded to unrecognizeable bits by stampeding buffalo hooves. The horse immediately puts Rosendo back in striking position and the hunter dispatches the animal with consummate skill.

The pungent smell of the kings of the plains is no longer recognizeable as horse and rider continue their teamwork until, after running about three miles, Alazan begins to tire. Rosendo will not risk injury to his horse so he reins Alazan out of the herd. The plains monarch is not as fast as a good buffalo horse but he has much greater endurance.

Rosendo had lanced at least twenty bison, a good day's work by any *cibolero's* standards. Man and rider were breathing heavily, both were still in a high state of excitement as they watched the buffalo speed by. But enough was enough. Man and horse had challenged the brute force of the king of the Great Plains and had won. There would be another encounter after all the buffalo meat was processed.

Alazan pranced as the last few bison ran away, rearing slightly and pawing the earth, showing his mettle. Rosendo patted him and said, "*Eso,* good boy." He looked around quickly and counted the horsemen. He saw only four at first but then the other two came into view. Fallen buffalo dotted the prairie. Rosendo took his flat straw hat in hand and waved it, signalling that everything had gone well. The other hunters did the same so there had been no casualties this day.

Rosendo Robles was the *mayordomo,* the *comandante* of the group of *ciboleros* and their crews. Each group had its own leader but there had to be one individual with authority to settle any dispute which might arise. Rosendo Robles was the authority this year, as he usually was, because of his hunting, diplomatic, and business skills. Hispanic *ciboleros* were freedom loving, independent individuals involved in the most dangerous sport ever practiced on the Great Plains, lancing buffalo from horseback, but it was also a necessary business to obtain meat for the people back home. One or two hunters could have done as they pleased but a large group of two hundred men needed central coordination in order to make the hunt profitable for all.

Rosendo knew his bison hunting well and loved the profession thoroughly.

Its challenge, rigor, danger, sport, and excitement were a constant lure for him when autumn began to creep onto the Great Plains. Though he was *el jefe,* the boss, he worked as hard as anyone when a job had to be done. Being *mayordomo* was only his final responsibility to the group for there was no salary involved. He had to hunt and work just like anyone else if he was going to make any money with hides or meat.

Alazan had barely quit prancing when Rosendo guided him to the first dead buffalo. "What a marvel you are," said Rosendo in Spanish as he dismounted and patted his steed affectionately. Then he took out his knife and began to bleed each buffalo he came to. Bleeding the animals was not the *comandante's* responsibility but he did it anyway because it had to be done and the sooner the better. Since he set the example the other hunters would follow it and everyone was better off in the long run. The hundred or so bison that had been killed were soon bled as it was the necessary first step in processing the meat.

"Good hunting," said Rosendo to his partner, Ambrosio Villegas, when they met to wait for the *carreros,* the wagon men who would cart the tons of buffalo meat into camp. It had indeed been a good *corrida,* run, for it was not quite ten o'clock in the morning, plenty of buffalo had been killed, there had been no casualties, and camp was not too far away. Already the whining wooden wheels of the *carretas* could be heard in the distance.

Rosendo and Ambrosio squatted down on the sod to roll cigarettes while they waited for the wagons. "You got some blood on your pants," said Ambrosio.

"Just a little squirt," muttered Rosendo as he tried to remove the stain with a dirt clod.

Ambrosio smiled wryly at his partner. The two were so different it was difficult for some people to understand how they had worked so successfully together for the past dozen years. Ambrosio was the bigger of the two though at first glance Rosendo looked taller because he was slimmer. Ambrosio was built like a giant tree trunk. His shoulders were enormous, his arms thickly muscled, his hands like buffalo hams. His chest was so deep he had never in his life been drunk, though he had tried time and again. Someone finally told him the size of his lungs neutralized the effect of the alcohol. His hips were almost as wide as his shoulders and his legs were so thick his trousers, like all of his clothing, had to be specially made. He spent much money on his clothes and he enjoyed dressing well, especially for dances.

Rosendo was lithe and well proportioned, almost two inches shorter than Ambrosio and not as powerful but quicker and more agile. He wore a flat straw hat, leather jacket and trousers, as did most *ciboleros,* and was muscular in the classical sense but in another time or place Rosendo might well have been mistaken for an artist or literary man, a chess master or a teacher of renown.

Ambrosio kept up a lively conversation which really was more of a monologue as the two men smoked their cigarettes. It was Ambrosio's nature to talk and discuss everything just as it was Rosendo's to weigh and consider silently.

Ambrosio was the acknowledged life of the outfit, always ready with a joke or story. He had travelled widely throughout the West while Rosendo was content to raise horses, training the best of them for the buffalo hunt, and farm his lands during the growing season. He knew the buffalo plains as well as anyone but he had never gone far and wide like Ambrosio who liked the plains, detested farming, and loved the mountains.

Ambrosio Villegas had roamed since the age of fifteen. He often accused Rosendo of sitting around the same orchard all his life. He liked to say that he had done everything there was to do in the West, *twice,* except for marriage, which he said he would never commit. People thought he had never stayed in one place long enough to form a permanent attachment with a female. He had met innumerable women in his travels, women of different races and rank, but his wandering lust had always been stronger than any attachment. "Mebbe I'll settle down when I get old," he'd say and off he'd go to the mountains to trap animals, on the trail to trade goods with the Comancheros, to his beloved Yellowstone Country for the sheer pleasure of it, to the buffalo plains for a hunt with Rosendo. "Ah, that Rosendo," Ambrosio would say to his friends, "he's a funny fellow. Hunting with a lance when he could be using a rifle! Yeah, I gave him a rifle, a good one. Probably gave it away or told his wife to hide it. A lance! That's a *man* for you."

Rosendo had liked Ambrosio from the first and their partnership had been a good one, a balanced relationship that had endured all stress. Rosendo Robles was a loner, a solitary figure difficult to know though the villagers admired him greatly as the best of the *ciboleros.* His horses were as good as any, his crops and orchards did well, and his buffalo hunting was a highly perfected art and business. He had a beautiful wife and four healthy children but unlike some *comandantes* Rosendo never allowed women or children in his caravans. He always brought his dog Lobo but he never encouraged others to bring their canines along. Lobo was half shepherd and half wolf. The dog had grown fast, eating meat and gnawing on buffalo bones. Lobo knew virtually everyone in camp, getting much attention since he was the only dog. Sometimes at night he would go out on the prairie to play with the wolves but he always returned to camp before daylight. During the day Lobo would bark thunderously if strangers approached the camp but at night he would not bark. Instead he would lick the face first of Rosendo then the other sleeping men in order to wake them up.

The two partners finished their cigarettes and went to help the wagon men load the carcasses after the entrails were taken out.

"When are you going to learn to relax?" grunted Ambrosio to Rosendo as the two men helped a trio of young wagon men lift some heavy green hides into a *carreta.* "When am I gonna stop working like a *peon?*" asked Ambrosio of himself. "*Hijo,* when I think of all the dances I've missed! To spend my life working like Robles, sweating like Robles. For what? ¡*Ay corazón*! I left my woman to dance with the buffalo!"

Every Hispanic village that sent out buffalo hunters would fete the men with a gala dance before they departed for the plains. Another festive dance would celebrate their safe return for dancing was an integral part of the

Hispanic culture of the Southwest. Rosendo did not care to dance and did it only rarely when his wife succeeded in getting him out on the floor. It was indeed difficult to find a Mexican that didn't dance but Rosendo Robles was exactly that.

Predictably, Ambrosio Villegas was just the opposite. He loved to dance. Ambrosio didn't spend much time thinking about things cultural. For him everything was the way it was and it didn't matter why it got that way. Dancing was one of his favorite activities and despite his bulk he was an acknowledged master of the dance floor. Ambrosio was never without a partner for women knew how well he danced and anyway they had been taught it was impolite to refuse a man a dance so long as he acted like a gentleman. At a Hispanic dance everyone danced with everyone, rich or poor, tall or short, fat or skinny. It was democracy in action and Ambrosio was a part of the action as long as *músicos* were playing. On a hot summer night his impeccable clothes would get soaked with perspiration so when the musicians took a break he would leave the hall, change into fresh clothes, and return before the next tune started. Ambrosio never stopped to think that the dance hall was a cornerstone of the Hispanic culture in the Southwest. He loved to twirl and embrace his partner, waltz and polka with her, joke, laugh, and be witty. There was nothing to compare with the sparkle in a woman's eyes. Ambrosio would ride twenty-five miles out of his way just to go to a good dance and he assumed unconsciously that everybody else would too. Almost everybody would have. Except Rosendo. It was ironic the two had met at a dance but then meeting strangers at dances was not uncommon, except of course for Rosendo, who seldom attended because he didn't much care to dance.

"I think we should go into Denison," said Rosendo to Ambrosio as they rode from *carreta* to *carreta* to see if anyone needed help, "after we put up the meat."

"I'll go tonight," said Ambrosio.

"After we put up the meat," emphasized Rosendo.

"Of course," said Ambrosio. "You think I'd miss out on all that butchering? Not a dance, eh, chance. You know me, shoulder to the wheel, nose to the grindstone, and a little foolin' around at Denison. Spreadeagle! No sense wasting a trip like that on you, Rosendo m'bye. Besides, there's guns in that town. No lances anywhere unless the Comanches decide to make a visit."

In one thing Ambrosio did not know his partner. Years before Ambrosio had tried to get Rosendo to stop hunting with the lance. He felt the rifles being used by the hidehunters would be much more effective and, despite the great expense, Ambrosio had given Rosendo a rifle and a sixgun.

Rosendo was against firearms because they were too lethal, too easy, too expensive. "They would take all the sport out of the hunt," he had said. He kept the rifle and sixgun but hardly ever touched them, at first. Then one day when the family was away he strapped the sixgun to his hip and tried drawing the weapon. He couldn't do it well and perhaps it became a challenge. Whenever he was alone he would practice and in time he wanted to shoot so he would ride away by himself and fire round after round, now with the sixgun, then with the rifle. At times he would practice drawing for up to six hours a day. He seemed to have a special talent for the quick draw and his shooting was fast, accurate, and deadly. He shot only at inanimate targets, never at animals, and the idea of a real gunfight seldom crossed his mind.

Rosendo never told anyone he liked to shoot or that he had a quick draw and a deadly shot to follow it. His wife saw him taking his weapons out for a day of shooting but she never thought it had any particular significance. The weapons and all ammunition were carefully hidden from the children so they were unaware of their father's hobby. But Rosendo realized that somehow firearms had become a part of him, especially the sixgun. It was as if the palm of his hand enjoyed slapping into the pistol butt as his thumb pulled back the hammer and the trigger finger set off the deafening explosion which resulted in a bullet burying itself in a target. Was the gun merely a new toy or something that had touched an inner chord, a basic drive, an obsession released? Rosendo wasn't sure. He never displayed his guns the way he did his lance but his firearms were always with him when he went out on the plains, though they were not used for hunting.

Ambrosio had the belief that his presents were all but forgotten. He would have been delighted to see how well his partner could draw and shoot but he never even suspected Rosendo could hold his own with just about anyone who wore a sixgun. Some of the men in camp owned firearms, including Ambrosio, but none were used in the hunt. They could have been used for defense but the size of *cibolero* camps would prevent most enemies from attacking. Lances, arrows, and knives were no match for firearms but Rosendo's diplomatic skills had always been sufficient to avoid major confrontations with Indians or hidehunters.

The *carretas,* about fifty in number and containing three times as many men, were about ready to cart the buffalo back to camp. The five-foot wooden wheels made a terrible noise that Rosendo found unbearable. It was the only part of his profession he would change completely if he could. Ambrosio didn't seem to be bothered as much as the two men rode to each wagon to see if anyone needed help in the loading.

"Good hunt," the wagon men said to the men on horseback.

"We'll have a fiesta tonight," said Ambrosio.

"After the sweat," finished Rosendo. Getting the meat back to the camp then processing it was no simple task. After the strain of the loading and unloading was finished each group would work the animals their hunter had felled. In an emergency the men of one village might help those of another but in normal situations every group was responsible for itself. Everyone worked, from the *mayordomo* like Rosendo to the greenest novice on his first trip to the buffalo plains.

Much of the meat was cut into strips and hung up to dry to make *charquí,* jerky. Some meat was smoked over a fire of buffalo chips, thus giving it a peppery taste. Some of the cuts were soaked in brine then smoked much the way pork was cured. The tongues were a delicacy and most groups preserved them.

Rosendo saw to it that no part of the buffalo was wasted. After the flesh was converted into jerky or cured, the fat was cut into large chunks and rendered into tallow for use in cooking and candlemaking. The crunchy *chicharones,* lardmeats which remained after the tallow was drained, were carefully stored for long winter nights goodies for the children back home.

Hides were converted into highly prized robes, skins, and rugs. The hides had to be scraped free of all flesh then kneaded with application after application of buffalo brains. They were labored over for ten days until they were soft and pliable. Robes had the hair left on but tanned skins had it removed. The work was tedious but the results paid handsome dividends for a top grade robe would sell for as much as $16.50 in a big city like New York.

Well formed horns were sought for ornamental purposes and the long wool from the neck and shoulders was gathered for later use in mattresses or for spinning into strong cloth.

There was so much work to do in a *cibolero* camp it was no wonder the groups were so large. Most veteran *ciboleros* had a specialty which they were particularly good at but everyone had to be able to do anything if the situation demanded it. There were hunters, freighters, skinners, knife sharpeners, cooks, butchers, hide handlers, guides, novices, friends and relations. Any individual with a good reputation and a sponsor was allowed to join the *cibolero* caravan if he vowed unconditionally to obey the *comandante* in all matters brought to his attention. In everything else he was more or less on his own. Business interests or family back home kept him serious and hardworking.

The first men to break away from the meat processing were the cooks who prepared meals for each group. Only breakfast and supper were prepared for the *cibolero* plainsmen for the day was spent laboring. Needless to say, the cooks had a great deal of informal authority because they prepared the meals. Rosendo always took care that cooking equipment like a big coffee pot, frying pans, and dutch oven were the best available, for a hungry man was often an irritable man. He believed in the old proverb, *Panza llena, corazón contento,* and sought always to take the best cook he could with him onto the Great Plains. Rosendo did not like to cook since his wife was one of the best but Ambrosio could easily have taken the place of any cook in camp. His duties as a hunter did not allow him to stay in camp too much but Ambrosio always worked with whoever Rosendo hired and taught him how to cook the hump ribs and other cuts which the big man loved so well.

The cooks were adept at their art and with the addition of vegetables like beans, chile, and rice, there was no better eating anywhere on the plains than in a *cibolero* camp. Sometimes the various cooks would try to outdo each other by preparing foods not commonly found in camp but usually the food was buffalo meat and vegetables. Biscuits were not rare so long as there was enough flour but cornbread was seldom available. Coffee and sugar were staples but they were also highly sought trade items for the Indians. Rosendo also made it a point to take along plenty of the oven baked crisp bread which the Comanches and other plains tribes loved so well. This item was strictly for trade or winning friendships with the Indians.

HEARTLAND

As the afternoon sun waned into twilight the cooking fires of buffalo chips were going strong, burning slowly with more glow than fire but ideal for cooking. The aroma of roasting buffalo meat filled the large camp. Visceral meats like the heart and liver were cooked immediately for the novices who could become ill on a diet of nothing but buffalo meat. They soon learned not to neglect their beans, rice, or corn.

Rosendo and Ambrosio were usually the last to sit down for supper, but this day everything had gone so well they could eat right along with the rest of the crew.

Lobo suddenly stood up from where he had been gnawing on a bone. He growled deeply, then barked thunderously. The men in Rosendo's crew looked up from their meal, peering in the direction that Lobo indicated. Three riders were coming toward camp. They were too far away to see who they were but within a few minutes it was obvious: hide hunters.

Men who preyed on the buffalo for skins were not difficult to identify. They were usually as bearded and shaggy as an old buffalo bull, their clothing stiff with dried blood and tallow. Their talk was as rough as it was loud from weeks and months of being almost alone or from yelling against the wind.

"Probably looking for a place to sleep," remarked Rosendo as he nodded toward Luciano and Anastacio, his most experienced hunter apprentices. The two men had thereby been assigned the duty of keeping a watchful eye on the visitors, rifles at the ready, so long as the strangers were in camp. Both apprentices understood their assignment and if Rosendo touched any part of his jaw with a closed fist there would be two guns aimed and ready to fire at the intruders, depending on what moves they made. Everything was prearranged but to all outward appearances the camp was involved in eating supper, nothing else, as the three hide men reined their horses to a halt about thirty yards from where Rosendo and Ambrosio stood.

"Howdy! " yelled one of the horsemen. "We're headin' down yonder and it do look like suppertime has kinda crept up on us. If'n ye got a little extry grub we'd shore appreciate it."

"Climb down," suggested Ambrosio as he waved the men in. "There's always food where there's buffalo." It was an unwritten law of the plains that everyone was welcome in camp so long as they didn't have mischief in mind. But some years ago Ambrosio had been refused admittance into a hide hunters camp on the charge that he was an Indian. Ambrosio had spoken English, Spanish, and a smattering of French to prove he was not Indian but he had been ordered away at gunpoint.

"We thank ye," said the spokesman. He appeared to be older than the other two. "Come on boys," he said so only his companions could hear him, "these greasers know how to be hospitable and nobody can't deny it. Keep an eye cocked."

Lobo growled deeply as the three rode into camp and dismounted. "*Está bien, Lobo, está bein,*" said Rosendo. The dog stopped his growling and laid down about ten yards from the strangers, his eyes riveted on them, his body relaxed but ready to spring instantly.

The three men were unacquainted with formalities and they were very hungry, so they served themselves large helpings of anything offered them and ate with savory gusto.

"Where you from? " asked Rosendo, who was nearly as fluent in English as Ambrosio.

"Anywhere I hang my hat is home," said the older man. "Been on the plains nigh on twenty-too many years. I guess I'll die here. Good a place as any to have your scalp lifted." There was no malice in the man and he smiled as he talked. Despite his shaggy beard and hair he was likeable. His companions, younger men but fully grown, didn't say a word as they ate. "You folks been working the buffalo very long? "

"Yes," said Ambrosio, "we hunt every season."

"Ye got a big outfit," said the man. "I seen your people hunting with the lance roundabout."

"Ever try it? " asked Ambrosio.

"No, I got my trusty old 'Poison Slinger,' I don't need no lance. By the way, this here food is right ways dee-licious. We shore do appreciate your hospitality. My name is John Williams," he said as he rose to shake hands with Rosendo and Ambrosio, who also introduced themselves. The other two men were Ben Watkins and Joe Starke.

"Why do you boys hunt with a lance? " asked John.

"Because we don't wanna sling no poison," said Ambrosio as he smiled. Watkins and Starke stopped eating momentarily. Their reaction didn't escape Rosendo's notice but he gave no outward sign of his awareness.

"That's what I call my Sharps .50," said John. "You ever seen one of them? It can fire eight times a minute and throw a bullet five miles. Let me get it from my horse so you can have a close-up look-see." He put down his food and fetched the rifle.

Ambrosio was familiar with the big buffalo gun but Rosendo had only heard them booming on the plains.

"This shoots today and kills tomorrow," said John Williams proudly as he set the rifle down.

Rosendo put his food aside and picked up the weapon. "This is a cannon," he said. It weighed sixteen pounds, much too heavy for use from the saddle but obviously effective when shooting from cover.

"That'll kill ye any buffalo bull at six hundred yards," said John. "Ben there likes the Remington and Joe is partial to the Henry but I'll take my Sharps every time. Mebbe you want to compare 'em." The other hide hunters did not move from their food. "Ah, after supper," added John. "Ye can take a few shots in the mornin' if ye have a mind to."

"Sounds good," said Rosendo, "and you can have a go with my lance if we find some buffalo."

John merely smiled. "I ain't never done no lancing. Too slow. How many buffalo you kill today? "

"About a hundred," replied Ambrosio.

"How many hunters? "

HEARTLAND

"Six or seven."

"Gee-rusalem! I've gotten that many all by myself with the Sharps." John was smiling all the while.

"We don't just take the hide and tongue," said Ambrosio in a matter of fact voice. "We use the whole animal."

"Sounds like Injuns," said Ben Watkins. "Buffalo is easy hunting. Stupidest animals I ever saw. Stand around and let you wipe out an entire herd."

"They're magnificent animals," contradicted Rosendo. "They've survived everything nature could throw at them and come out on top. The meat is better than beef."

"We take some of the choice meats too," said John, "iffen there's a market for 'em. I've knowed meat jerkers who could cut a whole hind quarter into one big sheet of meat."

"There's always a market for meat," said Ambrosio.

"There's a quicker market for hides," said Joe Starke as everyone was finishing supper. "That is, if yer interested in making money." Starke stopped eating for a moment. He scratched a shoulder with one hand, a leg with the other, and rubbed his side with an elbow. The bed rabbits had gotten hold of him. Rosendo and Ambrosio knew that Starke was a novice, for any plainsman of experience would have put his sleeping robes on an ant hill to get them cleaned out.

"We wouldn't be in business if we didn't make money," said Rosendo.

"I thought you hunted just to feed your family," said Watkins.

"Yeah, that too," replied Rosendo.

"And it's the best sport in the West," added Ambrosio.

"Sport! " exclaimed Watkins. "We ain't interested in sport. I came to make money! "

"What fun is slaughter the way you boys do it? " asked Rosendo.

"Slaughter is slaughter," said Watkins. "You lancers kill the animals, don't ye? We just kill more of them, that's all. Money is all the fun."

"Them buffalo is stupid," added Starke as he continued to scratch himself. "Fun is the last thing they be."

"To kill a buffalo and leave him to rot is a crime," said Rosendo.

"Says who? " asked Watkins.

"There's so many of them we could never kill them all," said Starke.

"Takes a man to hunt with a lance or a bow and arrow," said Ambrosio bluntly. "Takes guts to get up close and give the animal a chance to defend himself. Killing from a mile away, all that takes is a powerful rifle."

"And we got that," said Watkins. "But you ain't sayin' we don't have guts, are ye? "

"If it's yer horse, ride it," replied Ambrosio as he smiled.

"What guts does it take to kill an animal from a mile away? " asked Rosendo. "Tell me."

Ambrosio was surpised at how much conversation was coming out of his partner this evening. *El jefe* just didn't talk that much. Maybe he didn't know his friend as well as he thought.

52

"Guns and rifles aren't a test of courage. You have to get up close where you can touch an enemy with your hand if you have guts."

John Williams had been silent for the past several minutes. "But remember," he said finally, "yer enemy has a gun too an kin pick you off from afar."

"The buffalo aren't the enemy," said Rosendo, "they have horns, not guns. They deserve a fighting chance. An animal can't be an enemy. Buffalo were put here for a purpose. To kill them and not use them is very wrong."

"We use 'em," said Watkins. "There's too many anyway. Someday we'll bring cattle here and we can't have buffalo eatin' up all the grass."

"Buffalo are cattle," said Ambrosio. He was beginning to dislike Watkins.

"Injun cattle, maybe," said Joe Starke, "not for whites."

"Why not? " asked Ambrosio.

"Cattle are more intelligent critters," said Watkins. "Goldamned buffalo just ain't part of the plan."

"They're part of our plan," said Rosendo, "just like cattle and horses. And they're important to Indian families too."

"Injuns and Gre–," Watkins didn't finish. There was a heavy silence for a moment.

"I've seen it all over," said Ambrosio in a nonchalant conversational tone of voice. "Wherever your people go they destroy all the animals. Seems like you ole boys just can't stand to see something running around free. Ye gotta kill it to be happy. But then in a little while you're not happy anymore. So grab your gun and go kill something else."

"Well sir," said John, "guns we shore do have." John liked conversation for he had spent many a week alone with just the wind for company. But he didn't want to rile his hosts or their hospitality as the meal ended. He needed to make camp for the night and this one afforded ready-made security. "We sure do appreciate the food. We thank ye and tomorrow we'll shoot some buffalo for you if ye like."

"Yup," said Watkins, "two things buffalo is good for, killin' and eatin'."

"What does it feel like," asked John, "when you stick that thar lance in a buffalo? "

"Have you ever seen one up close? " asked Rosendo.

"No, not really," replied the hide man.

Rosendo went to his tent, brought out his favorite lance, and handed it to John. The scabbard was decorated with a multicolored tassel which dangled at the end of the leather case. John removed the scabbard, exposing the long, razor sharp blade which had downed many a running buffalo.

"Not bad," said John Williams. "I guess there's a lot to be said for a knife, iffen you know how to use it."

"Takes guts to come up close," said Ambrosio, "in buffalo huntin' or anything else." His comment wasn't intended as a challenge but the visitors didn't seem to appreciate it, Rosendo noted, especially the man named Watkins, who had a .44 strapped to his hip. But somehow the man didn't look as if the sixgun was natural to him.

HEARTLAND

"Ye can't beat a gun," said John Williams, "up close or afar."

"The man behind the weapon is still what counts the most," said Rosendo, "no matter what the weapon is. Look at what the Comanches have done against the army."

"They'll get rounded up on a reservation," said Joe Starke, "jest a matter of time."

"Probably true," answered Ambrosio, "but there are just a few thousand Comanches against millions and millions on the other side. Not exactly what you'd call an even match-up."

"True," said John. "Say, you fellers mind if we stay in camp tonight? We three shore ain't no army and them Comanch ain't the friendliest people in the world."

"Make yourselves at home," said Rosendo.

"Anybody for a bit of gaming with the dice? " asked Ambrosio.

"Now yer talkin' my language," said Ben Watkins.

After the dice were inspected and found satisfactory the game started and as it progressed the stakes kept getting hihger. Rosendo merely watched for he was not a gambler. Ambrosio began winning and his luck held throughout the evening.

"I need a drink," said Watkins. He and Starke went to their saddle bags to get some liquor. They couldn't help but wonder if the bones were rigged somehow.

"Ye ever seen a Mexican that lucky? " asked Watkins as he fished out a bottle of Double Anchor whiskey.

"Not hardly," replied Joe. He found what he was looking for in the whiskey he always carried, Pike's Magnolia.

"I ain't seen no guns on 'em though." Starke winked at Watkins.

"Must be some around somewhere. Course, greasers are knife people."

"Even Injuns can get back a-ways and shoot arrows into ye," said Starke after a long swig of the Magnolia.

"Well, I ain't never seen much difference between Injuns and Mexicans, myself." He took a long drink of his Double Anchor. "Come on, Joe, let's get our money back."

The two men returned to the glowing campfire where Ambrosio was in high spirits. "Whacha got there, Taos Lightnin? " he asked.

"No, that rotgut can kill ya," said Watkins. "I wanna get back in this here game."

"Suits me," said Ambrosio. "What else you have you wanna lose? "

"Those dice," answered Watkins. "How about these bones for a change? "

Ambrosio inspected them and pronounced them acceptable. "Ceptin' I don't like to beat a man with his own dice. You know how they make rotgut? "

"There's a number of recipes," said John.

"Worst rotgut I ever saw was at Fort Union on the Yellowstone," said Ambrosio. "They'd throw in a quart of alcohol, a pound of rank black chewing tobacco, a handful of red peppers, a bottle of Jamaica ginger, a quart of black

54

molasses and enough water to fill up the kettle. They'd boil that devil's brew until the tobacco and peppers were weak, then bottle the stuff. Enough to kill anybody, that rotgut."

Watkins and Starke drank their whiskey and won for a while but then Ambrosio started winning again.

"Thunderation! " said John Williams. "I guess I'm snake-bit tonight. I quit."

Starke quit after a few more throws and Watkins won a little. He decided to wager everything against Ambrosio's throw and lost when the dice rolled an eleven.

"Well, I ain't! " exploded Watkins. "These dirty Mex—"

Ambrosio struck Watkin's forehead with a clenched fist and the man fell over like a sack of potatoes. Joe Starke was almost as drunk as his friend but he did nothing. Neither did John and their inaction definitely saved their lives.

Ambrosio stood up as if nothing had happened. He picked up his winnings as he cast a glance at Watkins. Rosendo was with Williams and Starke, trying to revive the fallen man. Lobo growled deeply from a few yards away. Watkins had a large bump on his forehead, dangerously close to his eyes. If the blow had landed on the nose it might have been fatal but Ambrosio had not intended to kill.

"Lucky punch," mumbled Starke.

"Shut up," ordered Williams, who had not done much drinking and was in control of his senses. "Hot tempered numbskull. Seven kinds of fool he is! Goldamned tenderfoot is the reason we got stranded anyways. Sorry," he said to Rosendo, "to repay your hospitality like this. When men gamble and get likkered up there's always trouble. I know, I've been there. But some men have no business on the plains a'tall."

A wet cloth was put on Watkins forehead. He revived after a few minutes but was still incoherent.

"You can put your bedrolls by the fire," said Rosendo.

"We won't cause no more trouble," said John. He hoped the Mexicans wouldn't try to collect their firearms. They wouldn't be given up just for the asking though he was hopelessly outnumbered.

"You can keep your guns," said Rosendo, much to John's wonderment at the timing of his remark, "so long as you don't pick them up unless we get attacked during the night." It was a reasonable compromise for John. But was Rosendo making a mistake? Would the visitors cause trouble during the night? It would be suicide for them but was it worth risking the lives of any in the *cibolero* camp?

"It was just the likker," said John. "We didn't come for no trouble."

Rosendo nodded and walked over to Ambrosio. "Don't worry about 'em," said the big man. "They're not killers, just gore and slaughter hide men. You can always tell a killer by his eyes, an icy blue with a lighter ring at the edge of the iris. Killer eyes. Backshooters and murderers. A whitish ring where color should be. Men without a soul. I've seen 'em."

Ambrosio had always been careful in fights for with his great strength he could easily kill someone. But he wasn't a killer. He had no reason to like hide hunters after what had happened years before in one of their camps. In all trouble with English speaking people he had learned to strike the first blow when a fight was unavoidable. With his strength that was usually as long as the fight lasted: one blow. He had also seen that many who spoke English natively were usually racists and bigots. While he was not much given to reflecting on cultures he wondered why certain types of people considered themselves better than Indians or Mexicans. So many English speaking people who came West were little more than tramps who lived miserably. Oh, some of them had courage all right, but few showed it if they didn't have safety in numbers or plenty of guns and ammunition. Well, those types had better watch out. Ambrosio didn't need anybody's acceptance, particularly, but he would demand respect. And if he didn't get that he would extract fear. He looked at Watkins and said, "Well, time to hit the sack. Work like a *peon* all day and more of the same tomorrow. There must be a better way to earn a living. *Buenas noches.*

The camp settled down for the night amid the weakening glow of dying cooking fires. The *ciboleros,* tired from their constant labor, slept soundly. There were no incidents during the night and the only sounds were the howling of wolves in the moonlit distance or an occasional neighing of camp horses. Far away from the *ciboleros* a cow leader got an unfriendly scent in the wind. The cow lifted her head, swung it this way and that as her nostrils flared. She turned and began to move, her head down in a determined march. One after another the bison fell in behind her, then other little bunches. In a long string they wound up around some breaks as the land rose to a high table. There, beyond all water, they marched into the wind once more as the great herds had been doing since the beginning of time.

Rosendo was already up when the call of the meadowlark and the whistle of the bobwhite greeted the dawn. He kindled a small fire and set the coffee pot on it. Lobo kept him company for the dog had not gone out to play with the wolves. A few coyotes let out their yelps and in the remote distance a wolf howled but all was stillness before the dawn. Rosendo thoroughly enjoyed the few minutes before sunrise, for it renewed him spiritually much as sleep did his physical body. When his coffee was ready he sipped it slowly and merely gazed at the orange horizon. A stranger would have thought the *cibolero* was meditating, but he wasn't, for this was about the only time of day that he permitted himself the leisure of doing absolutely nothing. Lobo came up to him and licked his hand.

"*Vagabundo,*" said Rosendo, "you decided to stay in camp last night, eh?" He looked over to where the three hide hunters were beginning to stir. "I'm glad you stayed," said the man.

"Thanks, master," said Ambrosio as he walked up behind Rosendo.

"*Buenos días le de Dios,*" greeted Rosendo.

"What are you going to do when Lobo finally does talk to you?" asked Ambrosio as he poured himself some coffee. The cooks for the various crews were beginning to start the day.

"It's all right, so long as he makes sense."

The large camp was now awake and soon everyone was busy working the meat. The cooks had breakfast ready in an hour. The hide men ate some food then went on their way. Watkins seemed to be all right but quiet. John Williams thanked Rosendo and Ambrosio before departing.

At mid-morning Lobo barked out the alarm that strangers were approaching. Two horsemen were riding toward camp and leaving a trail of dust behind them. As they approached it was obvious their horses had been ridden hard for a long while. The two riders seemed to be making a desperate dash toward the camp but the horses were reined up suddenly and halted in their tracks. The men talked to each other then allowed their horses to walk toward camp.

Ambrosio went out to meet them. The riders were not hide men. They were well armed and both had blue eyes with coldness staring out of them. Ambrosio turned toward the camp as he rubbed his chin with a clenched fist.

"Howdy," he said as he smiled.

"How do," said one man nonchalantly.

"Seen any signs of Comanche? " asked the other rider.

"Nope," said Ambrosio. "You lookin' for them or them for you? " he asked, a broad smile on his face.

Neither of the horsemen replied. "Let's go," said one of the riders as he cast a contemptuous look at Ambrosio. The two horsemen rode away from the *cibolero* camp and were soon lost in the horizon.

An hour later a Comanche war party of seventeen men loomed out of the horizon. Once again Lobo had thundered the alarm. The warriors seemed to be studying the camp as Rosendo cautioned everyone to continue working after they hid their weapons close by. The *comandante* could not make out what band the Indians belonged to as the warriors walked their horses toward the *ciboleros*.

About a hundred yards away from the Hispanic camp the Comanches stopped and only one warrior continued forward. Rosendo said to his men: "Don't make a move unless I give the signal," and walked out to meet the Comanche spokesman.

The warrior rode a spirited pinto pony that pranced more than walked. The Comanche saw the Hispanic coming forward alone and on foot. A smile worked its way across the warrior's face and he clasped both hands in front of him, the left hand under the right. Rosendo made the same gesture:

— Peace.

The Comanche dismounted and walked to Rosendo. The warrior held his right hand across the left side of his chest, the thumb and index finger making an incomplete circle, then he raised his hand even with the shoulder, folded his arms across his chest then raised both hands until his fingers pointed skyward. Then he held his hand palm down, thumb close to his left breast and keeping his arm horizontal, swept his hand outward and a little to the right:

— Good morning.

Rosendo knew he was being tested so he repeated the greeting. Then he made the signs for:

HEARTLAND

     – You are welcome in my camp.

     The Comanche held his closed right fist above his left palm and made a circular motion as if turning a crank:

     – Coffee.

     Rosendo nodded.

     The Comanche leader continued:

     – We search for two bad white men.

     – Hide men?

     – No. Killers.

     – Two white men went by here.

     – When?

     – One buffalo skinning ago. Over there are the tracks.

     – Good. I return for coffee.

     – What will you do?

     – Drink.

     – No, with the white men, signed Rosendo as he smiled.

     The Comanche brought his nearly closed right hand sharply down and across from his shoulder, stopping it with downward extended fingers in a vigorous rebound:

     – KILL.

     The warrior mounted his prancing horse and made the peace sign before dashing back to his comrades and leading them to the tracks made by the fleeing whites.

     Rosendo waved goodbye when the warriors let out a warwhoop. He walked back to camp and related what had transpired.

     "I hope they catch 'em," said Ambrosio. "I knew they were killers the minute I saw 'em. The eyes give 'em away every time."

     Everyone returned to their various jobs. Besides drying great quantities of meat the workers also cured much of it for sale later on. Each group would dig its own square hole and line it with a fresh green hide, pegging the edges to the ground at the rim of the hole. The cavity would hold up to a thousand pounds of meat which would be salted and left in the hole from seven to eight days. Then it would be taken out and washed as thoroughly as possible. Next it was hung in a smokehouse made of poles and hides. A fire was made in a small hole in the ground, green wood being used whenever it was available though buffalo chips and grasses were more accessible fuels.

     Most hunting groups brined the tongues and packed them in discarded whiskey barrels. The tongue was a delicacy and brought in good side money. But if the tongues were eaten in camp they were boiled until tender then fried in the marrow of the big bone of the buffalo hip.

     Buffalo hump was the basic meat eaten in the *cibolero* camp. The meat was darker and fatter than beef and many hunters preferred buffalo to beef. Rosendo was particularly fond of hanging the hams of fat bulls in a mesquite tree at the beginning of the *cibolero* season, then going to pick them up weeks later toward the end of the hunting. By that time a crust had formed and the flavor of the meat was at its most savory. The meat was sliced across the grain, salted lightly, and fried in a skillet.

Buffalo fat also made an excellent base for a mouth-watering gravy. Barbecued ribs were also delicious eating in a *cibolero* camp. Everything seemed to taste better on the plains and if buffalo meat was cooked with skill there was no better eating anywhere. Appetites built up on the buffalo plains were also whetted by the fact that there was no meal served at noon.

After the days of processing the meat were done Rosendo mentioned to Ambrosio: "I think I'll go into Denison and bring in more supplies. We're running low and the Comanches will be back sooner or later."

"I'll go with you," said Ambrosio. But then he reflected and added, "No, I guess I'd better stay and take them out on another hunt."

"You can go if you want," said Rosendo. "I'll stay and hunt."

"No, I've been to the Palace and the Sazerak. Nothing there I care to see again. Besides, maybe you'll drop by, just for fun. Do you some good, eh? " Ambrosio laughed for his partner didn't care for dens like the Palace.

Indeed, Rosendo would never even think of going to Denison if Lobenstein of Leavenworth didn't have an agent there for purchasing buffalo hides. Then too, if the Lobenstein agent didn't pay well enough Rosendo could barter his hides and robes at the big General Store on Main Street.

"I'll get some wagons ready," said Rosendo. "About how many hides do you think we have ready to go? "

"I don't know. No problem though. We have plenty of wagons." Ambrosio thought a second then said, "Make sure you take the rifle and the .44. Course, I don't know what you'd do if you had to use either one."

Rosendo wrinkled his forehead and ignored his partner.

Word spread throughout camp that Rosendo was going into Denison and most of the crews decided to send a wagon with hides and bring back supplies. A total of nineteen wagons would make the trip into town. With Rosendo Robles to drive the bargain everyone thought they would do well.

The wagons were packed with hides and supplies for the trip. There would be only one man per wagon but he would be well armed with firearms if possible, knife and bow and arrows a certainty. Only Rosendo had a rifle, pistol, and knife.

"We'll see you in about a week," said Rosendo to Ambrosio as dawn colored the sky the morning of departure. He strapped on the gunbelt and pulled out the sixgun a few inches before jamming it softly back into the holster.

Ambrosio looked at Rosendo and the familiarity with which he handled the sixgun. The belt and gun looked perfectly normal strapped on the *cibolero*. Ambrosio and the other men were unaccustomed to seeing him armed that way and thought it strange but the departure began when Rosendo climbed into his *carreta* and signalled the mules to move out.

"*Vaya con Dios,*" said Ambrosio. "Be careful you don't shoot your toes off."

The wagons set out, whining, creaking, grinding their way across the prairie.

HEARTLAND

By the second day out the little caravan was making good time as dawn greeted the *ciboleros*. The air was pure and not even vapor streaked the emerging sun. For a few minutes the *ciboleros* could see the vast expanse of prairie. The deep blue of the horizon was the only fence that existed as away in the distance a little cluster of antelope were grazing in a ravine as it slowly filled with sunlight. Bands of wild horses could be seen gamboling on green hillsides. Here and there a wolf or coyote had not finished its nocturnal rounds. The landscape was rich in stands of bluestem grass, pokeweed, and sagebrush. The caravan came to a creek bordered by a thin strip of woods, mainly cottonwood, hackberry, willow, and plum trees with a sprinkling of chinaberries and skunk brush. The creek and greenery of trees had attracted wild turkey, prairie plover, and quail which flew or scattered at the approach of the *ciboleros*. Some wild ducks and geese also took to noisy flight.

Along about mid-day the caravan encountered hideous reasons why hidemen were so thoroughly hated by the Indians and a growing number of *ciboleros*. Eighty-eight buffalo carcasses gleamed a sickening white in the sun, the glassy eyes staring into nothingness. Rosendo stopped to inspect the animals but it was as he thought: only the hides and tongues had been taken. The thousands of pounds of meat had been left to rot and the air was already becoming putrid.

Rosendo felt the sixgun at his side and for a moment wished he could find the hide hunters responsible for this carnage. What savages, what barbarians these hidemen were! What kind of a society produced such killers, such waste, such wanton destruction? Perhaps Ambrosio was right: the hide men were driven by insatiable greed, they delighted in gore, and understood only force brute and bloody. Something had to be done. The buffalo would not last forever and without them there would be no more *ciboleros* or autumns on the plains. But what to do? *Help the Comanches* was all he could think of as he climbed back in his wagon and continued toward Denison.

When the caravan reached Denison the next day Rosendo had calmed down. He had a gun and knew how to use it but his only thought now was to get the best possible price for his hides. It was unlike him to flare up angrily and deep inside he still smouldered but right now he wanted to make a sale.

Denison was a typical frontier town with more than its share of thugs, gamblers, and loose women. Hogs wallowed in mudholes in every part of town that didn't see continuous heavy traffic. Skiddy Street, one block south of Main, was lined on both sides with tents and shacks that housed low class bars, gambling joints, cocking pits, and hurdy-gurdy dance halls. The most notorious dives in this town of dives were the Palace, the Sazerak, and the Park.

The *ciboleros* reined their wagons to a halt in front of the largest general store on Main Street and Rosendo went in to inquire if the Lobenstein agent, a man named Miller, was anywhere about. The hunter learned from one of the customers in the store that Miller had been drinking at the Palace a short time before so Rosendo left the store and instructed his men outside to guard the wagons while he went to fetch Miller.

Rosendo made his way down Main and turned on Skiddy Street. He walked into the Palace, which was not well lighted even during the day. Rosendo's eyes had to get accustomed to the twilight atmosphere but this was accomplished momentarily. He made his way to the bar and ordered a beer.

"Have you seen Mr. Miller, the Lobenstein agent? " he asked of the bartender when the beer was served.

At first the bartender merely looked at Rosendo. "Two bits," said the man behind the bar.

"I've got a load of hides for him," continued Rosendo as he put the money on the counter.

"You a hide man? " asked the bartender after he picked up the money.

Rosendo thought of the sickening carcasses which were stenching the plains by now. Eighty-eight tributes to barbarity and greed. The *cibolero* took a long drink of beer. "I've got some good hides for him," he said.

"Miller, ah, Mr. Miller stepped out for a minute. I expect he'll be back directly," said the bartender as he went on to another customer.

Rosendo had finished his beer when Miller walked in through a back door, a fancy woman on his arm. Miller's face was even redder than Rosendo remembered it. The man's lady friend wasn't as red but she was a heightened shade of pink, Rosendo observed as Miller went to the other end of the bar. The bartender went to the man, told him something in a voice too low for the *cibolero* to hear, then Miller looked in his direction and came toward him.

"You lookin' for me? " asked Miller.

"Yes, *señor* Miller, I have some quality hides for you again, at a very good price."

"Ah, Robles, sorry I didn't recognize you. How's it goin' this year? "

"Fine. We have quite a few hides for you over by the General Store," said Rosendo.

"Okay, let's get a drink first then we'll see wha'cha got. What are you drinkin', beer? Let's have a whiskey and a beer over here, George."

The bartender brought the drinks over and set them down in front of the two men.

"*Gracias,*" said Rosendo as he lifted the glass as if toasting the agent. He brought the drink toward his lips but he never tasted the beer for two thunderous shots rang out and two bullets ripped through Rosendo's back and churned like a bloody plow through his heart. The beer splashed against his face but he was dead before he jolted into the counter and crumpled to the floor.

A deathly silence took over the Palace as the beer glass rolled off the bar and smashed itself on the floor. The only movement in the entire room was the ascending, ghastly blue smoke from the acrid barrel of the .44 which was held by a lone gunman who stood some twenty feet away from the bar.

"Thunderation," exclaimed Miller as he looked at the gunman then at Rosendo's corpse. The others in the room suddenly realized a shooting had taken place and moved as far as possible out of the line of fire. Several individuals bolted out of the bar altogether.

HEARTLAND

"That there's a wanted man," said the gunman, his sixgun still in hand. "Name's Silva. Swore to kill me any way he could."

Miller had not moved since the shooting. The gunman returned his .44 to its holster but he kept his hand on the weapon. Other men began coming toward Miller and the corpse on the floor.

"I don't know if he's wanted," said Miller, "but his name sure ain't Silva. It's Robles. He's a buffalo hunter. I've had business dealings with him before."

"The gunman stepped forward, his hand still resting on his pistol butt. "You sure?" asked the man as he turned the corpse over with his booted foot.

"I'm sure," said Miller, "and he's got a big outfit."

"Lemme have a drink," said the gunman to the bartender, "whiskey."

The sheriff was sent for and arrived quickly.

"It was an accident," explained the gunman to the sheriff. He related how this Mexican bandit named Silva had bushwhacked some innocent settlers, been captured by the U.S. Marshall but broken jail before the hanging. "That stiff on the floor is a dead-ringer for that Silva. It was an accident, pure and simple."

There was no one around to contradict the gunman's story and the cadaver couldn't talk. The sheriff had little choice but to accept the gunman's story.

"Probably a horse thief anyway," said the gunman as he finished his whiskey.

"Any next of kin around? " asked the sheriff.

"I don't know of any," volunteered Miller, "but he said he had some hides for me to look at over at the General Store."

"Well, I guess I'll go tell 'em about the accident," said the sheriff. "Why don't you mosey on out of town, just to avoid trouble," he said to the gunman. "No sense startin' a race war over this."

The gunman said nothing but he walked slowly out of the Palace.

"I'll go with you, sheriff," said Miller, "to look at those hides."

"Hey, what'll I do with this carcass? " asked the bartender.

"We'll tell the others," said the sheriff. "They'll probably want to bury it."

"That was a little too close for comfort," said Miller to the sheriff as the two headed toward Main Street and the General Store. "For a minute I thought I was next . . . ."

VI

THE ADOBE ABODE

"How soon will we get there, Dad? " asked five-year-old Sean as the scenery hurried by at fifty-five miles an hour.

"In about half an hour," replied the father. "Don't be in such a rush. Look at those beautiful *mesas*. See what a beautiful world we live in."

"I want to see Gramma," said Sean. "Will she have some goodies for us? "

"Yes, *lindo*," said the mother, "Gramma always has goodies for you and your brothers."

"Why is that mesa red in the middle? " asked Christopher, the eldest of the three brothers.

"Different layers of the earth have different chemicals in them," explained the mother, "and that causes different colors. See that mesa, how yellow it is? "

"Chemicals," repeated David, the second oldest son. He thought a while then said, "But where did the chemicals and everything come from? "

"They think the earth blew off the sun," explained the mother.

But David wasn't satisfied. "And the sun and the stars, how did they get made? "

"From a combination of all sorts of gases."

"And God put them all together? " asked Christopher.

"Well, where did God get the gases? " persisted David.

"I know where," burst Sean, "from the gas station! "

When the hilarity subsided the parents continued to point out the beautiful scenery to their children. The multicolored mesas combined with rolling hills and the gleaming highway to achieve an enchanting and hypnotic effect on the boys. The grandeur and majesty of the scene never diminished though the family made the trip many times.

"There's the *pueblo*," said the father. "We're just a few miles away now."

"Yes, and we have to go through another Indian pueblo, huh Dad," said Christopher.

HEARTLAND

"Yes. Would you like to stop on the way back and maybe talk to somebody from the pueblo? "

"Are they friendly Indians? " asked Sean.

"Aah Sean, don't be such a baby," ordered David. "Indians are just like anybody else. They don't shoot people anymore. So I don't want to stop."

"I'm not a baby, you're a baby," accused Sean.

"Look Sean," counseled the mother, "your friends Robbie and Tina are Indians. Are they good people? "

"Are they Indians? " asked Sean. "I like Tina but I'm going to marry Jennifer."

"Some Indians are good and some aren't," said Christopher.

"Just like every group of people," said the father. "We come from Spanish-Mexican people and some are good, some not so good, just like Indians and everybody else."

"My teacher said that Indians stole horses and everything," said Christopher, who was in the fourth grade, "but they didn't know any better."

"Sure they stole," said the father, "but only from their enemies. They never stole from their own tribe. If you could go steal a horse from your enemy everybody thought you were a great warrior. They didn't think of it as stealing because they were at war. When we go to war we take things too, don't we? All these lands belonged to the Indians and we just came in here and took them."

"Why didn't all the Indians get together and throw out everybody? " asked Christopher.

"Cause nobody ever told them they were Indians," said the mother.

"What? "

"Sure, before Columbus came to America the people here weren't Indians. They were Pimas, Navajos, Zunis, Apaches, Sioux, Cherokees, and all the other tribes. Then the Europeans came and put them all in the same group by calling them 'Indians.' But they were all different, just like the Europeans. If the Indians had all been together, united, the Europeans would never have been able to conquer them"

"We're Spanish, huh Mom? " said Christopher.

"Our ancestors came from Spain through Mexico but we probably have an Indian or two back there somewhere."

"Jennifer is an American," said Sean. "I'm going to marry Jennifer."

The bronze station wagon was making good time across the hills and countryside. The three boys let out some yelps when they saw the school which was situated on the outskirts of the tiny village.

"There's the big adobe house! " yelled Christopher as if he had sighted a rare spectacle.

The imposing structure looked as permanent and natural as the mountains north of the village. The adobe walls had the same brown color as the earth while the woodwork of doors and windows was bathed in a sunshine yellow. The pitched tin roof reflected the fading afternoon sunlight right back at the heavens as the car passed through the open gate into the yard. The boys romped over everything as they tried to get out of the car until their father ordered them to behave. Before everyone was out of the car a short, elderly grandmother came out to greet them. She was smiling lovingly and drying her hands on her apron as she came toward the car.

"*¡Nanito! ¿Cómo están mis hijitos, a ver?*" she said as she bent slightly to hug all three boys. Her great-grandchildren returned her warm embrace.

"Gramma, do you have a goodie?" asked Sean.

"*Si, nanito,*" replied Mama Juanita as she embraced the father and mother, asked them how they were, said how glad she was to see everyone, and told the family to come inside the house. All conversation was in Spanish while the children yelped in English.

"I was expecting someone today," Mama Juanita said as she brought dishes out of a cabinet in order to set the table for supper. "I was hoping my *hijitos* would come to see me before school started again. What, *nana*? Yes, I've been sick lately, my back." Mama Juanita always complained about her health although there were some people who believed her to be one of the healthiest people in the state. Her energy was unbelieveable, especially for her seventy-eight years. She had been known to plaster the outside of her home, by herself, paint every room on the inside, and even move heavy furniture around. Once some of her relatives found her atop the house fixing the tin roof! When asked how on earth she got up there she replied simply that she had used a ladder borrowed from a neighbor.

"I'll give you a rubdown tonight, Mama," said the mother.

The car was unloaded while supper was prepared. Mama Juanita had no difficulty in preparing food for five extra people. In her day she was considered the best cook anywhere, this during a time when a woman was judged by her children, religiosity, cooking, and housekeeping. The boys washed their hands and trooped to the supper table where they devoured the meal with typical gusto.

"Can I have some more pears?" asked David.

"May I," said the mother.

"May I?"

"Yes, but you can finish your milk first."

"Why are pears a 'may' and the milk a 'can'?" inquired David as he scrutinized the milk.

"Young man," threatened the father.

"They don't speak Spanish yet, *hijo*?" asked Mama Juanita.

"Oh yes, Mama," quickly replied the father, "they understand quite a bit of what I tell them. But I guess they can't speak yet. Where we live we're the only ones who can speak another language so the kids hear nothing but English all the time. Except from me."

"What a shame," said Mama Pita. "I wish they could speak Spanish so they could stay with me for a while. I'm alone all the time now. I don't even have any renters during the summer."

"You should come live with us."

"Yes, I will one of these days, but if I leave here there will be no one to take care of the house. By the way, when you rest up a bit I'd like you to see if you could fix..." She mentioned a few jobs which need to be done..."after you've rested."

"Yes, Mama, I'll attend to them tomorrow."

After supper the boys were allowed to play outside the yard. They quickly met other children and the whole crowd went into an orchard, picked up a few rotten apples, and started throwing them at each other. When Sean came in crying and rubbing a sore spot on his thigh it was decided that bedtime had arrived.

"But I'm too tired to rest," protested Sean. The three dynamos were soon in bed, however, after they had extracted a promise from their father that he would take them on a hike the following day. With the boys tucked away the grownups could talk to Mama Juanita.

"And how do the old days compare with today, Mama? Would you like to go back? "

"No *hijito,* I don't think so. People had to work too hard. When I was a little girl we had some Indians who helped with the work so my older sisters didn't have much to do. But later as I was growing up we came upon harder times and I became the Indian. I had to bring water from the stream and dirt with which to plaster. I think that's when I first started having trouble with my back. Today you don't have to work as hard, so I think life is better now."

"You wouldn't want to go back? "

"Never," said a very sincere Mama Juanita. "I worked more than a pair of oxen. Today you have machines to do all the work. People work and make good money. I can remember when a man would have to work a ten-hour day for a dollar-and-a-half. No, the good old days were more like centuries of backaches. The women today put the clothes in the automatic washer and then say they're tired. How ridiculous."

"And the people, are they the same as always? "

"No, the people are very different. They don't have any love or pity for anyone. Yes, the old people are put in homes because the children are too busy working to take care of them. They can't be bothered anymore. If someone in the neighborhood is hungry nobody cares or does anything about it. Everything is money and machines. A person today doesn't have a soul, just a bank account. No, life is easier today but a lot more wrinkled."

"But I thought you liked machines."

"Yes, I do, but not more than God. Only people can get you to Heaven, but few persons seem to realize it. I wonder why that should be? "

"Everyone is the way God made him, and often a good deal worse," said the grandson. "Cervantes said that."

"Cervantes? Yes, there was a teacher who once rented the house here. Taught at the school for a year. What did he say? "

"It's not important, Mama," said the granddaughter. "Come on, you're very tired, let me help you to bed."

Good nights and pleasant dreams were wished on the younger generation by the elderly, wrinkled, stooped humanity who was growing progressively harder of hearing, weaker in health, and more grand by the day.

"That little old lady is really something," said the husband as he and his wife prepared for bed.

"Oh, don't call her that."

"And she's not just talking about people in the neighborhood going hungry. I remember when I was growing up, about eight or nine. One evening we had just finished supper, a regular feast like always when we came to visit. The table was cleared and everybody sat around talking. Mama Juanita saw this guy, I don't know who he was. She sent me after him to invite him to come in for supper. He was walking aimlessly down the road. I caught up with him and told him my grandmother wanted him to come in and have supper. He sort of mumbled somthing unintelligible as we both walked back toward the house. He looked kind of funny to me. You know, I was just a kid. He walked funny, sort of with a choppy bounce and his hands dangling from his wrists. He must have been mentally retarded or crippled in some way, I don't know. But Mama Juanita smiled at him and told him to come in and have supper. She gave him the very chair she had been sitting in and the same kind of food that everybody else had eaten. The room full of people just talked while the man ate. I stayed to watch him instead of going out with the other kids. I don't know why. When he finished he went out the front door just like when he came in. I don't even remember him saying 'Gracias' or anything, although I'll bet he did. Mama Juanita didn't say 'Was it good?' or 'Come back tomorrow' or anything like that, just '*Pase buenas noches*' like she said to us. I followed the guy outside and watched his funny walk down the road . . ."

The following morning was begun by the stomping of three sets of feet which would have chased off any wild mustang adventurous enough to dare competition. The boys stampeded onto their parents' bed, pranced around on it, and were finally bucked off by the grownups who were trying to sleep. The boys dressed then went outside and onto the street in search of action.

"Hey, who lives in those houses with the smoke coming out? " asked Sean.

"Probably people," said David the devilish as he picked up a stone and hurled it at a fence post.

"I know that, but who? " said Sean. "You missed. I can throw better than you."

Christopher's large brown eyes opened wide. "Hey look! Here come two cows! " If the entire village didn't hear him it was only because it was no longer interested in war whoops or battle cries. "Maybe we can ride 'em! "

The three warriors charged at their chewing, disinterested prey.

"Now don't panic," Christopher stated for he was the acknowledged strategist of the group. "Sean, you stand in front of them while David and I get on 'em."

Sean's facial expression began to doubt Christopher's genius. "Gee, they have horns," he observed.

"Don't panic," ordered David.

"I won't," snapped Sean, "but what if the cow does? "

HEARTLAND

Christopher grabbed one of the cows by the tail as David ran his hand along one of the cow's backs.

"Shall I get on? " asked a hesitant but excited David.

"Yeah! " yelled Sean just as David flung himself more on the cow's side than her back. The sudden yell and assault were too much for old bossy. She kicked her feet, snorted, burst out in a run. Sean scampered out of the way as Christopher's cow pulled him for ten quick yards until he lost his grip and crashed to the road. David managed to stay on his cow for a few seconds but when she bolted sideways David landed squarely on his back, the air being knocked out of his lungs. He writhed and gagged as his two brothers walked over to him.

"Breathe me, breathe me! " gasped David.

A boy and girl came out of their house and raced to the fallen David.

"You hurt? " asked the other boy.

Within a few minutes David was laughing along with everybody else since minor bruises often became the medals of boyhood warfare. The new boy and girl were Duane and Margie. The boys invited them to go on the hike they had planned and Duane said he could show them a path up through some cracks in the mountain. The idea of a cracked mountain filled the boys with wonder and enthusiasm.

"Come on with us, Duane," said Christopher. "We'll have breakfast then my dad promised he'd take us. You too, Margie."

The five children walked back to the adobe house where the grownups were preparing breakfast.

"Come in, *nanitos*, come in," said Mama Juanita. She greeted Duane and Margie and invited them to have breakfast but they said they had already eaten. The parents of the boys finished the preparations for the breakfast of hotcakes and served the boys who devoured their food as if they had been working since sunup. There was no peace until the father and the five children were on their way toward the tablelands that were situated east of the village.

"Duane, are you sure you know a way up? " asked the father as he looked at the perpendicular side of the mesa.

"*Sí, señor,*" replied Duane, "we can go up through the cracks. I do it all the time."

"Okay," replied the incredulous adult. He had played all over these mesas when he was growing up and he didn't remember any path. As they made their way to the mountain side the father asked Margie and Duane various questions during the course of their conversation. He learned that Duane had passed on to the sixth grade "en condishun," that there were fourteen children in the family, and that one had died recently. It turned out that Duane didn't particularly care for school. The father looked at the youngster's dark skin, listened to his accent, and wondered who his teacher was and how he viewed this boy. He was a teacher himself and he remembered how his teacher colleagues ridiculed accents that came from languages other than English and, in a subtle way, any student with a dark skin. Sean's skin was about as dark as

Duane's and the father wondered what his "educated" fellow teachers would say about him.

"See, we go up this crack," said Duane.

"Up there? " asked Sean.

"Now don't panic," said Christopher. "Come on."

The group went up a large crevice where the rock had split apart for three or four feet. Pieces of stone had fallen or chipped off, thus affording varying steps for the ascent. Why had the rock split? What if it happened to split now or move just enough to send another boulder crashing down? Sean began to whimper.

"Come on Sean," said his father, "I'll raise you up." The small boy had to be lifted up for a step that was taller than he. He was swung up and when he almost lost his balance his large black eyes watered.

"I want to go home now, Dad," he said as he struggled against the tide.

"Don't panic. I'll take care of you," consoled the father in an effort to conceal a chuckle. But he didn't want a rock to fall either.

"Just a little more and you're out of the crack," yelled Duane. He and Margie scaled everything like mountain goats.

The two older boys were out of sight as Sean and his father climbed the last steps out of the crevice. They were waiting out in the open air but clinging to the side of the stone mesa.

"Oh, here we are! " said a relieved Sean as he left the crevice. But then he looked down and the tears began to roll with very little resistance. The village seemed far away and a possible fall was so close.

The next step was so high everyone except Duane needed to be lifted. When it came to Sean's turn he wouldn't allow his father to raise him and let go.

"Okay," said the man, "I'll put you on my back and we'll climb like we did at the ruins. Now don't panic and let go."

Sean tried but he was whimpering and almost wailing with each swaying motion of his father's back. He held on so firmly he was restricting his dad's breathing. "Don't choke me, Sean," gasped the man.

"I don't want to climb anymore! " wailed the five year old. The tears were flowing freely by the time the top was reached.

"Now see? " said the father. "Look at that beautiful view. Wasn't it all worth it? "

"Yes," agreed Sean, "and I'm glad I didn't panic."

The village lay nestled miles away in the distance. The road snaked its way through the miniature town, around hills and over streams of silver, toward black mesas and green pastures where cattle seemed to be the size of insects.

"Hey Dad, let's build a little campfire," suggested David.

"It's not cold," protested the father, not appreciating the interruption from the panorama before him.

But everyone else wanted a fire so he consented. The man pulled a book of matches out of his pocket as the children gathered some wood. They quickly

HEARTLAND

accumulated enough for a small fire but there was no paper with which to start it.

"Pine needles," said Duane, "we don't need paper."

David said, "If you want the job done right, do it with pine needles," as he gathered all he could.

The fire was built and enjoyed. The children ran behind this tree and that while the father relaxed and surveyed the world of his boyhood. How far away the screaming sirens, the jetting airplanes, the ulcers, the modern world, *civilization.* Yes, he was in favor of wonder drugs but not junkies. He wanted technology to make life better but what about pollution? He would not want to wash clothes by hand at the river but neither did he want polluted water or poisoned air.

Mama Juanita said there was a lack of love. Had there been mass murderers before, mass hate, mass mess? Where had all of society's wrinkles come from? And was he helping with the solution or was he an integral part of the problem? He was in debt, paying off house, car, stereo, appliances: the great American rat-race dream. But if you don't have those things you feel like such a bum. It doesn't matter if you're just one jump ahead of the sheriff. Declare bankruptcy and let the creditors go hang. Hate thy neighbor as thyself? 'Give me your tired and your poor.' 'Why don't Negroes go back where they came from?' 'Chicanos have to work their way out of their poverty. They can't just stay on welfare.' What hangups society had!

But yet he felt himself an American through and through. He liked this person or disliked that one but it had nothing to do with money and social class. Or was he lying to himself? Who was he to resist the teachings, the dictates of his society? There was only one commandment: Thou shalt not be poor. Only one crime: getting caught. But he couldn't go back to — what? The absence of television? Could he make it without hamburgers? Without hate, polluted air and water, traffic jams, mistrust, fear?

What would he do, come back to the village and take up farming? He'd starve to death. What kind of education would the kids get? What kind of a job would he find? Build his own house? 'Four rooms and a path?' No, he couldn't go back.

VII

LIBERATION

General José Castro looked out the window of his office then back at the indignant face of *Don* Sebastian Peralta as the facts concerning the horse-stealing episode were related.

"And when I told him the horses were to be returned immediately," said Peralta, "or he would suffer the consequences, he spat a stream of tobacco juice at me and said I could kiss . . ."

"I understand, I understand," finished Castro. "I have observed the behavior of the men with Lamont." The general wrote out a note for the justice of the peace then handed it to Peralta. "Take this to the *alcalde* and the matter will be resolved shortly."

"They are heavily armed," advised Peralta as he made his exit.

Castro merely nodded. United Statesians are always heavily armed and looking for a fight in this day and age, he thought. Consul Tarkin was in the employ of the United States and would favor an American takeover, of course, and a California independent of Mexico was not an impossibility; but that high-handed, bragging Lamont wanted a gringo California and *that* was not desireable. Castro lit a cigar as he thought. He finally concluded that Lamont and his adventurers must be ordered from the country. A gringo California?! Perish the thought. They were supposed to have said the new California would throb for literature and the arts, that a new republic unlike any other would be forged by new men from east of the great mountains and plains. All they had accomplished so far was to steal horses and spread rumors. No, California could do without Lamont and his crew of roughnecks. He, General José María de Castro y Sosa, would see to it.

So it was that on February 20, 1846, the *alcalde* of Monterey summoned Lamont to appear in court to explain the horse stealing charge. At first Lamont took it as a joke and laughed heartily. Then suddenly he became deadly serious and felt grievously insulted. He, Timothy William Lamont III, a captain of the United States Army, appear in a contemptible greaser court? He called his men together to relate the communique. The nerve of these Californio greasers! Let's see what his patriots would say.

"Men," began Lamont in his most eloquent style, "this little scrap of paper I'm holding in my hand could mean war, revolution! You all know why we're here: to protect American lives and property. We must never forget the women and children who have only us to face danger and injustice . . ." Lamont talked for several minutes and got the group into a patriotic mood. By the time he mentioned the horse stealing charge the men were ready to drag Castro out of his office and lynch him.

"Are you willing to lay down your lives for your beliefs? " yelled Lamont.

"YEAH! " was the response from sixty lusty throats.

Lamont wrote a curt reply to the summons, saying he did not have to appear in any California court, that his accusers were liars merely trying to sully his good name.

On March 5 Castro replied to Lamont: he and his men were to leave California immediately or they would be driven out.

"Hear that, men? They're going to drive us out like a flock of sheep! " Timothy William Lamont III knew a cause when it trampled him.

"I figger tha's goin' to take a heap a doin'," hollered one individual clad in buckskin.

"Let's drive *them* the flock out of here! "

"Them greasers sure talk a good fight."

"Lay it on 'em, Captain! "

The men were ready.

"We'll give ole Castro a lesson in tactics," said Lamont. "See that hill over yonder? " He pointed at Gavilan (Hawk) Peak. "Let's break camp and fortify that big rock. Then we'll see if Castro wants to do some shearing! "

WHOOOEEEEEE! yelled the jubilant throng as the men looked at the peak then at their leader. It was indeed a brilliant tactic. The whole Mexican army couldn't dislodge them from it, not in a million years.

The expedition marched to the top of Gavilan Peak, built a crude but solid log fort, named it "Fort Liberation," and raised the Stars and Stripes over it.

WHOOOEEEE! yelled the throng as the American flag waved in a gentle breeze. The fat was in the fire: Castro would have to attack to chase them out of California. Lamont could see for miles in any direction along the Royal Highway and his position was impregnable.

Two riders were spotted coming down the road and a volley of rifle shots rang out, mostly to inform them where the action was. The riders, probably army scouts, made a hasty retreat.

"You bring Gen'ral Castro with ye next time ye come, fellers! " yelled one of Lamont's men. "I'll personally curl his wig six ways from Sunday! "

"They'll be back, men, with plenty of friends," encouraged Lamont. "Keep your rifles at the ready. We don't want to lose because of some sneaky greaser surprise." Lamont was as cool as a brook trout under a willow root, but nevertheless he sent a hurried note to Consul Tarkin, assuring him that all the men in the expedition vowed to die for the liberation of California, that if their force was attacked by overwhelming numbers, he, Captain Timothy William Lamont III, would die at his post.

When Tarkin read the note he thought Lamont must have gone stark raving mad. Die at his post? ! The Californios hadn't fired a shot! If Lamont wasn't careful he would ruin the carefully laid plans of the United States! "Headquarters in the saddle," Lamont had finished his note. *He's confused his brains with his headquarters,* thought Tarkin. *If I send somebody out there he'll probably shoot him. We'll just have to wait and see what happens.*

Meanwhile, back at the peak, Lamont and his men waited for the Californios to attack. It didn't come the first day, the second, nor the third. By the fourth day the expedition was short of food and almost totally out of water. The men began to grumble and fight among themselves due to the inactivity. Maybe the greasers had outsharped 'em? They could sit on Gavilan Peak until Satan shook hands with St. Peter for all the Mexicans cared, eh? What a brain struck idee it had been anyway! Lamont must have slipped his head hobbles. This was worse than being in the middle of hell with the lights turned off.

That evening Lamont gathered the men to inform them of his latest tactic. "Fellow countrymen," he said, "the greasers know they can't dislodge us from here. Their only weapon is starvation. But they ain't gonna beat us. If they're too cowardly to attack we're gonna take it to them." He gave the order to break camp and sheepishly hauled down the American flag. He then marched his men east through the coast range and into the San Joaquín Valley. After saying he was heading toward Arizona he returned to Sutter's Fort, this being an effort to confuse his pursuers, though unknown to Lamont there weren't any because the Californios hadn't gotten around to giving him the attention he sought. Through it all Lamont believed his tactics were as bright as a fresh minted penny.

Shortly after the Gavilan Peak episode, Tarkin was visited by a Lieutenant Archibald H. Winston, a courier from the U.S. government who ratified verbally the status of Tarkin as a secret agent in California. But Tarkin's secret written orders had arrived safely so there had been no real need for Winston. However, it so happened that he had a packet of letters for another party.

"Who? " asked Tarkin.

"A man named Lamont."

"Heaven help us! " exclaimed Tarkin. "I was hoping we'd heard the last of him. Who are the letters from? "

"His father-in-law," replied Winston, "the Senator from Tennessee."

"Well," shrugged Tarkin as he pointed out the window toward Gavilan Peak, "he went that way."

Archibald H. Winston was not one to shirk his responsibilities. He rested for a few days then set out in pursuit of Lamont. He trailed the expedition to Sutter's Fort, learned it was supposed to go into Arizona (though no one knew why or what for) but that in reality it had marched toward Oregon (and again, no one could tell why). Winston finally overtook the group in May of 1846 while it was camped on the shores of Klamath Lake just over the northern boundary of California in the Oregon Territory. The tenacious Lt. Winston delivered the letters to Lamont, satisfied that he had completed his duties.

Lamont did not discuss the letters from his senator father-in-law. When some of his right hand men and fellow patriots asked him about them all he said was that they were written in "secret code" and had to do with very delicate matters. He gathered the members of the expedition and told them they were no longer going to Oregon, that Arizona was out of the question. "We are needed in California," he told his men. "We must safeguard American lives and property wherever found. We must be ready to do our duty for our country. We must be *discreet* but we cannot let foreigners take over California. We must be first . . ."

At that instant rifle fire claimed two men as they fell over dead. The Klamath Indians would have no invaders around their lake and warwhoops filled the air. Lamont's men were taken by surprise and many arrows buried themselves in human flesh but only two men were killed before the expedition counterattacked and forced the Indians to retreat due to superior fire power. The Klamaths had possessed very few firearms and bows and arrows were no match for rifles.

In retaliation, before departing for California on "delicate matters" and trying to be as "discreet" as possible, Lamont ordered that the Klamath village be burned to the ground. A village was located, though no one thought to ask if it was Klamath, and the orders were carried out. If the conflagration was not delicate or discreet enough, the heavily armed expedition marched down the Sacramento Valley hell-bent for — something.

On June 10 Ezekiel Sterritt and some of the boys ran across Lt. Francisco Arce* and three of his soldiers.

"What ye doin? " asked Sterritt.

"Gathering horses for General Castro," replied Arce.

"Boys, I don't see no reason why a bunch of greasers should be collectin' horses to organize a cavalry. Anybody wanna help me run Arsay's arse into San Francisco Bay? "

There wasn't one dissenting voice. The men raided Lt. Arce's party and took all the horses it had collected after running off the outnumbered soldiers with a volley of rifle fire. The animals were delivered to Lamont's camp on the Sacramento River.

The entire camp became delighted with the excitement.

"Now let's see what General Castro does! "

"I hope he comes alookin' for his horses. We'll send him ass over teakettle right into the bay! "

"Think he's man enough to fight? "

"He'll be all shriveled up and curly cued after I gits through with him! "

Lamont encouraged the jubiliation but he realized he was in a ticklish situation. He knew his men were the stuff heroes were made of but didn't want to go down in history as provoking a war. Another council was called and in true democratic fashion everyone was allowed to speak his piece.

* AHRR-seh.

One of the first men to talk suggested the expedition take over all of California north of San Francisco Bay.

"If we controlled Sonoma we would control the whole north," observed another. The patriots accepted the idea immediately so it was decided to attack the garrison there and take over the town.

Lamont decided to remain in camp along with some reserves in case Castro decided to attack. He promised to swoop in like an avenging angel if resistance at Sonoma was tougher than expected. His rhetoric was enough to give any native Californio the dry shivers, if there had been any around to listen.

Sonoma was a tiny hamlet at the northern end of the Royal Highway. It was the site of a garrison and the mission San Francisco Solano de Sonoma. Dawn was still a couple of hours away when thirty heavily armed gringos crept into the tiny village, ready to catch the garrison by surprise. The barracks were completely dark and the invaders knew that victory was in their grasp. They surrounded the building, rifles ready to ring out for freedom. Not a greaser was stirring anywhere!

After a whispered conference, the leaders of the attacking force decided to charge right in the front door and take charge. Ezekiel Sterritt, Bob Temple, John Grigs, Bill Ade, Will Hart, and Lyle Smith jammed their way through the door and Sterritt boomed out: "SURRENDER OR DIE! "

Nothing moved.

"Wake up! This here's war! "

Still nothing crawled out of bed to surrender.

"Light a match real careful like," ordered Bill Ade. The soft amber light was enough to show the heroes that the building was completely empty.

"Those godamned greasers! " exploded Grigs. It was Gavilan Peak all over again. Defeat had once more been snatched from the jaws of victory.

When the obscenities cleared up somebody said, "Well, at least we can capture the head greaser in these here parts."

"Who's that? "

"Mariano Vallejo. He lives down the road a piece."

Mariano Vallejo was Castro's adjutant in charge of northern California, as good a hostage as any. Dawn was beginning to color the skies when the liberating attackers surrounded Vallejo's house. Will Hart banged on the door with his rifle butt and hollered:

"Wake up in there! Come on out with your hands up."

Nothing happened.

"Come on, get up! "

After more banging on the door a sleepy-eyed, elderly man, slightly on the rotund side and obviously a servant, finally cracked open the door and peeped outside. *Dios mío,* what a mean looking bunch of plug-uglies greeted this dawn. The man closed the door.

"If anybody opens that door again and doesn't surrender, shoot right through it," ordered Bill Ade. "Light those torches! If they don't come out we'll burn 'em out."

HEARTLAND

Don Mariano Vallejo, the adjutant of northern California and still in his night shirt, opened the door.

"Is your name Vallejo? " asked Ade.

"At your service, señor," replied *Don* Mariano.

"You're under arrest. Surrender peaceably or forfeit your life. We have the whole town under our control."

Mariano Vallejo reflected momentarily but did not close the door. "Señores," he said, "It's an unusually chilly dawn for June. Would you not prefer to come in and discuss this matter over a glass of wine or perhaps some brandy? "

That sounded good to Sterritt, Temple, and Hart. "You boys wait here," said Temple to the other men. "Us three will get his signed surrender. If there's any tricks, fire the house, never mind about us." The foursome, led by the adjutant in his night shirt, went into the house.

"If only I had known you were coming I would have had breakfast ready," apologized *Don* Mariano. "If you will excuse me for a few minutes while I dress myself? Jorge will bring some wine and our special brandy. Jorge! "

"No tricks," cautioned Sterritt in a menacing tone.

"Señores, there is no need to concern yourselves. My house is your house." *Don* Mariano exited as Jorge brought a decanter of brandy and several bottles of wine.

The three liberators poured themselves some brandy, then some wine, then more of each.

"I wonder what's takin' him so long? " asked Temple.

"He'll come in all high shouldered and fancied up," said Sterritt after gulping down some brandy. "Not bad likker."

"Regular connysewer, ain'cha? " said Hart. "Let me do more sampling."

The ambassadors of the new California drank and waited while Vallejo dressed. *Don* Mariano brushed the dust off his uniform and put it on, sword and scabbard included. He looked at himself in the mirror and decided his side-whiskers needed combing. When he was satisfied with his appearance he rejoined his guests. He smiled broadly as he entered the room, sword clanking, and said, "I trust you will pardon my delay. But at least I hope our hospitality has not been found wanting. Jorge, more wine, *por favor.*

Tobacco juice spitting Ezekiel Sterritt began to speak but belched loudly instead. Vallejo merely passed him the decanter of brandy and Sterritt took it willingly.

Meanwhile, outside the house there were more than thirty rather impatient heroes waiting for an opportunity to show their mettle. They talked in small groups, glared at the house, paced back and forth, determined not to fall for any tricks. One of the groups was discussing the pros and cons of starting their own government but one independent individual wanted no part of any kind of government and let his feelings be known this way:

"Who needs a govmint anyhow? Buncha greedy fat bastids and tax men and parsons, that's all. I seen 'em. I been up in Pennsylvany and around. Fat polytishuns what know everythin' and glad to have a chance to tell you. You

80

don't hafta open your own mouth. They'll talk a mule to death. Politics, that's what they call it. Pig slop I say. Polytishuns! I never hope to see anuther cussed one. They smell like fancy clothes, big money and tellin' me what to do. I say the hell with 'em, the United States, the damned British and the parley-voos, too. Gimme western folks every damned time. I'd ruther get steel in my ribs, poisoned by bad whiskey, et by a bear or scalped in the woods before'n I take off my hat, lissen sweet, git talked to death, taxed outta what I got and then flung inta jail by them lyin' mouthed bastids."

An entire hour had gone by and still there was no sign of life coming out of the Vallejo house. John Grigs decided to go in and see what in thunder was going on. Grigs knocked on the door, knocked again louder, then again until Jorge came to let him in. The door closed once more and the armed heroes outside waited, paced, spat, and eyed the house with sullen impatience. Fifteen minutes dragged by, then twenty, thirty. After forty-five minutes had elapsed, Bill Ade spoke up, saying that something must be seriously wrong inside. Were Vallejo and his staff killing everyone inside, one by one?

"I wouldn't put it past 'em. Them greasers is treacherous."

"I'm going in," concluded Ade. He took his pistol in hand and made certain his large hunting knife was unencumbered. He knocked on the door, then rapped it several times with his gun butt. No one came to let him in. Swearing furiously he threw all of his weight at the door as he turned the knob. The door flew open on impact for it had never been locked at any time.

Ade crashed to the floor as the door rebounded against the wall and slammed shut again. Ade picked himself off the floor, pistol in one hand, knife in the other, ready with the spring of a tiger. He saw no sign of life until he identified some kind of movement to his left. He sank to one knee and pointed his pistol at what turned out to be a yawning pussy cat. The family cat walked out of wherever he had been sleeping and went to find a quieter corner.

Ade peeked into the parlor, saw nobody, then made his way to Vallejo's office where, ready for any trick, he saw what had taken place. Bob Temple, a huge man who stood six-foot-eight in his stocking feet, was sitting at Vallejo's undersized writing desk, mumbling to himself as he wrote something on a large sheet of paper.

"What in hell are you doin'? " Ade wanted to know.

"Writing the articles of capitulation," replied Temple as he looked up bleary eyed from his laborious, painstaking work. "How the hell do you spell *indemeninety — indemty — indam —* ah, piss! " he exploded as he reached for his drink, swallowed it in one gulp, then poured himself another. Temple began to mumble what appeared to be a scrambled version of the alphabet. "Ah hell, you write it! " he said to Ade.

Mariano Vallejo was seated at a table, smiling pleasantly, smoking a cigar as a servant removed the breakfast dishes.

Ezekiel Sterritt was seated across from Vallejo, his head in his arms on the table, sound asleep and snoring.

Will Hart was sprawled on the sofa. He opened one eye, looked at Ade, groaned loudly, then closed the eye.

HEARTLAND

Grigs, the last of the heroes, was lying on the floor, snoring peacefully, completely unaware that he was holding a smashed wine glass in his right hand.

Ade looked suspiciously at Vallejo, his pistol at the ready.

"The victors are preparing the articles of capitulation for me to sign," explained *Don* Mariano. "I shall be happy to sign as soon as I have read them. I don't believe we've met. I am Mariano Vallejo. Would you care for some brandy? "

"Christ! " groaned Ade. "What a way to fight a war! "

"Ah señor, war is unthinkable," said Vallejo. "We are all at peace here." Sterritt's and Grigs' snoring emphasized the remark.

"No, I don't want no brandy," said a determined Ade. "I'd better finish this here writin'." He took Temple's place at the diplomatic table. He reviewed the early chapters of Temple's work but it appeared the later ones had become rather cloudy. Ade labored until he finished the document in what he considered to be his best international style then he handed everything to Vallejo.

Don Mariano carefully set down his cigar and began reading. About halfway through he smiled and said, "I must apologize. I cannot read English very well. But I should be happy to sign this most remarkable document anyway. Could you pass me the pen and ink? "

Ade did so and *Don* Mariano signed. Grigs staggered to his feet and though reeking of brandy he had enough presence of mind to say, "Where's Lamont? He's gotta pass on this."

Ade took the document outside and read it aloud to the assembled revolutionaries. While he read, Sterritt, Hart, Temple, and Grigs staggered out of the house. "California is no longer greaser country! " yelled Ade when he finished reading. "We have to form a government at once. Nothing remains but to see this thing through."

The liberators yelled their approval. Because he had drunk no brandy, Ade was now the leader, much to the displeasure of the individuals who had done the work inside Vallejo's house, each of whom thought himself the leading patriot. But Ade was left in command at Sonoma while the others went to inform Lamont of the successful revolution. It didn't matter to them that Mariano Vallejo was more of a private citizen than a ranking government official when it came to representing California.

"First thing we gotta do is raise a flag," said Ade. He asked for volunteers to work on the project. When there were none he appointed Lyle Smith to do the job because he was a house painter. Smith decided to accept the responsibility and set out looking for suitable cloth. All he could find was an old petticoat of *Doña* Francisca, Vallejo's wife. "It'll have to do," said Smith. He began the historic work in front of the Vallejo home as the other revolutionaries went hither and yon in the tiny village.

"There," said a proud Smith when he finished his masterpiece. A breeze came up, causing the petticoat to flap about. "You," he said to one of the servants watching from the house, "come hold this out for me."

Jorge came out of the house to comply.

"What do you think of it? " asked Smith as he put on the finishing touch.

Jorge studied the creation. In the upper left hand corner was a five pointed star, at the bottom was a band of red, underneath it was written CALIFORNIA REPUBLC. But Jorge was most puzzled by the animal in the center.

"Well, what do you think? " repeated Smith.

"Why a pig? " asked Jorge.

"That's not a pig, that's a grizzly," said Smith as he shook his head. Jorge looked at it again but said nothing. "A bear is the strongest animal in California," explained Smith, "and he always stands his ground." Then he noticed he had left out the "i" in *Republic*. As he was correcting the mistake the breeze got stronger and a boy came out from the group of spectators to hold the cloth down.

At last the flag was finished. Smith looked at it with great satisfaction. "There you are, son," he said to his young helper. "You've taken part in one of the greatest events in the history of California. You'll remember it all your life. What's your name, sonny? "

"Vallejo," said the boy. "I am the son of Mariano Vallejo." As he went back into the house he thought gringos were certainly weird people to put a pig on a petticoat and call it history.

The Mexican flag was hauled down and up went the Bear Flag. "A bear always stands his ground," said Ade during the short cermony, "and as long as the stars shine we stand for the cause."

Lamont was delighted with the success of the Bear Flag Revolt and now he came forward to assume command of all military forces. He galloped here, there, and everywhere, consolidating his power and proclaiming a new era of freedom. He led a night attack on the presidio at San Francisco only to find it abandoned. The cannon were so old and rusty they might well have been brought by De Anza, but Lamont had them spiked anyway.

Ade resented Lamont's actions. "I pulled the chestnuts out of the fire just to have Lamont stomp in and munch them," he said bitterly.

Lamont labeled Ade and illiterate upstart.

Sterritt, Temple, and Hart resented both. "We were the ones who captured Vallejo and made him surrender," they said indignantly.

John Grigs was at outs with everyone because he felt his efforts had been slighted entirely.

No one ever mentioned that *Don* Mariano's house had been completely looted of all valuable belongings that could be carried away, though the avowed purpose of the revolt had been to establish a republic which would endure as a bastion of freedom, literature, and art.

No Thomas Jefferson emerged to write the necessary constitution and when the California Republic was twenty-five days old and on the verge of a bloody counter revolution a messenger reached Lamont at Sonoma with the news that the United States had been at war with Mexico since May 13 and what was this about some Americans who had decided to capture California and start their own republic? All the principals were ordered to come in and confer with American authorities at Monterey *at once*

HEARTLAND

The Bear Flaggers immediately went to pledge their allegiance to their country. Only the servants remained in the Vallejo house at Sonoma. Jorge was delighted to see Lamont and his men leave. In their haste they forgot their flag. Jorge looked up at it. "Looks like a pig," he muttered.

VIII

THE HILL
OF THE JEALOUS ONE

Tazbah looked up at the jutting black fingers which pointed to the sky-vaulted expanse from an otherwise calm Earth Mother. Her horse knew where they were going as he walked slowly toward the arroyo and crossed it carefully. Tazbah thought of the many times she and Poh seh tan had ridden their horses around the craggy black hills, the lake to the south, the tablelands all around. "Poh seh tan, Poh seh tan," she whispered passionately. "I am waiting for you. Don't be long for I cannot bear to be without you." The horse flicked his ears toward Tazbah but continued walking, realizing that the woman's passionate voice was not directed toward him.

Tazbah looked at the ground for signs of fresh tracks but found none. Maybe Poh seh tan was ahead of her already, waiting to surprise her along the trail. She was ready to feign surprise when he charged into her path, scaring her horse, while she pretended to nearly fall from her saddle. It was ridiculous to think that a woman descended from warriors could fall off her mount, but she would pretend even the ridiculous if it would tickle Poh seh tan. She looked at the three hills, all bunched together, that Poh seh tan loved so much. They were so much like the love they shared, she thought. They started on the level plain, went up into a small hill, then a larger, and finally the highest which was the summit of love, the threshold of eternity, the spirit world of Poh seh tan's love.

"May your evening be delightful," he had said when they first met around the fire at the Round Dance over a year ago. She had merely looked at him without replying. Pueblo men were so different from those of her own nation, not as fierce, not as free. But there was something about this man that Tazbah had liked as he walked by her so she looked at him boldly. If it was too much for him she might as well know it right away. The man did not seem to mind but he did not invite her to dance as he was doing with some Pueblo women. "Perhaps he prefers his own kind," she had thought to herself. "No matter. There were men and women in the world, Pueblo, Navajo, Nakaie, all of them

different in ideas." Tazbah looked at a little group of Nakaie away to her left. She didn't know any of them though they were probably villagers from the settlement to the north.

"Blue butterflies and honey bees must hum over a blossoming corn field," Tazbah heard someone whisper from behind her. She turned and the Pueblo man put a turquoise necklace around her neck and fastened it expertly. His sensitive hands brushed against her neck and hair for a fleeting, soothing instant, then he withdrew them.

Tazbah looked at the man and smiled softly. He gazed into her eyes where the bonfire reflected itself and warmed him inside. The spiderweb turquoise felt cool and caressing around her throat. *"May you ever walk in beauty,"* said Tazbah.

The two had danced the rest of the evening. Tazbah refused to dance with anyone else even when Poh seh tan was gone for a time. She knew he would return.

Tazbah's horse stumbled slightly, causing reality to lurch back into her consciousness. "Easy, careful," said the woman as the horse continued to walk. They were beginning to climb now. The small rock at the base gave way to larger ones as they went up. A fat lizard stopped to look at the intruders, then away before the monstrous shadow of horse and rider engulfed him.

Tazbah dismounted when she arrived at the large juniper tree. She and Poh seh tan had always left the horses by the juniper and gone on afoot because there was too much dangerous footing ahead and a horse could easily injure a leg. "Poh seh tan, Poh seh tan," she whispered softly. Tazbah decided to wait by the juniper where the scent was sweet and comforting. She sat next to a cactus flower that was full of pollen. The beautiful flower was yellow on the outside, orange inside where a honeybee was gathering pollen. Tazbah looked up suddenly when she thought she heard hooves in the distance but it was nothing. She felt a slight pull on her hair so she brought it over her shoulder but the rich black hair was so long it still touched the ground so she gathered it once more and laid it in her lap.

"Why is your hair so long?" Poh seh tan had asked the first time she had visited him in his workshop.

"Because I don't cut it, silly," Tazbah had replied as she smiled.

"Why, you could cover your entire face and most of your body if you combed it to the front."

Tazbah was still smiling as suddenly she bent forward sharply, her beautiful black tresses swinging over her head and covering her face when she straightened up again. *"La llorona of the Nakaie is going to get you, Poh seh tan."*

"Quit, you silly maiden," said Poh seh tan as he laughed and parted her hair to peek at her face. When his eyes met hers he crossed his and pretended great fright.

Tazbah giggled then burst into an uproarious laughter that didn't stop until there were tears in her eyes. Poh seh tan laughed as he put Tazbah's hair to the side, his hands caressing the raven black as laughter subsided.

THE HILL OF THE JEALOUS ONE

"You have beautiful hands," said Tazbah, suddenly serious. "You must be a true artist." She looked at the turquoise jewelry he had created. "Why didn't you tell me you made jewelry?"

"I am glad you like my work," said Poh seh tan, "but it is only a hobby. I like to work in my fields just as much. Then there are my horses."

"This is beautiful," said Tazbah as she picked up a bracelet, "like a plume wand."

"I will make you a gift of it, Tazbah," said Poh seh tan. "Tazbah. What a pretty name. How different it is. What does it mean in your language?"

"Descended from warriors."

"Descended from warriors," repeated Poh seh tan. "I had better be careful. I have heard about warrior women."

"Oh? What have you heard?"

"That they can be as fierce as they are beautiful." He took her hands in his and looked deeply into her eyes.

Tazbah took the man's eyes. How different they were, how soft, how caressing. "And what does 'Poh seh tan' signify?"

"Print of the morning dew," he said.

"Print of the morning dew. Poh seh tan. You name is as soft as a white floating cloud."

"Be careful. My people have a rain song named that."

"White floating cloud?" asked Tazbah. "How does it sing?"

"You expect me to sing it right here?" asked Poh seh tan with a mischievous look in his eyes.

"Why not?"

"A rain song in my workshop?"

"Yes," commented Tazbah, "unless your roof leaks or you sing so mightily that a flood would drown us away."

Poh seh tan laughed at being caught in his own joke, then he sang softly:

"White floating cloud,
your thought comes to me . . .
Cloud like the plains,
your thought comes to me . . ."

When the man finished singing Tazbah said, "You make a good song. I love the plains and the clouds."

"Do you like to ride?" asked Poh seh tan.

"Of course. My people are warriors and warriors must have horses. We have beautiful animals that rival those of Johano-Ai."

"I do not know this Johano-Ai."

"He is simple to know," said Tazbah. "Johano-Ai starts each day from his lodge in the east and rides carrying the sun to his lodge in the west. He has five different horses, all of different colors and hues. When the weather if comfortable he rides his turquoise horse, or the one of pearl or white shell. When the sky-vault is stormy he rides the horse of red shell or of coal. All the horses' hooves run on precious hides and blankets and when the animals gallop *they churn up flashing mineral dust which my people collect and use in ceremonies. The sacred horses feed on flower blossoms and drink holy waters from the four corners of the world. Without Johano-Ai there would be no sun."*

"I see," commented Poh seh tan simply. "You tell a beautiful story. You are a beautiful woman . . ."

Tazbah came out of her reverie and got to her feet. What if Poh seh tan had come up from the other side as they had done once. Here she was waiting on one side and he might be doing the same on the other! *That joker. That wonderful, wonderful joker!* Tazbah challenged the rocky climb as if she was a mountain goat. She crossed the dry, rocky arroyo that had cut a small gash down the hill. A few strenuous minutes later she came to the large piñon tree that signified she was half way up. Tazbah almost slipped to her knees because of a treacherous rock which looked solid but came loose at the pressure of her footstep. She watched the stone stumble and bump to the bottom of the hill. *"Poh seh tan, Poh seh tan,"* she thought, *"in some little hollow, in some low brush, reveal yourself to me, my love. I do not like climbing our hill alone. "*

Tazbah stopped to rest momentarily. She was slightly out of breath and hot. Johano-Ai was high in the skyvault as he journeyed westward. A distant cloud seemed suspended in the blue, a cotton softness on a bed of turquoise.

"You belong up in the sky, my beautiful white floating cloud descended from warriors," Poh seh tan had said when they met for the third time.

"How so? " Tazbah asked coyly.

"You should always let the universe see your beauty. The white light of morning is your smile, the red light of evening is your skin, your tears are falling rain, and your love is a standing rainbow. With you at my side it is fitting to soar where birds sing and walk where grass is green."

Tazbah's eyes shone brightly as she said, *"My own special one, I must tell you my heart. I love you, your voice, your footstep, your shadow. You have become a part of me and my spirit. If you took yourself away I would want to die. I will make you some bright beaded moccasins so that you will ever walk toward me, never away, never away."*

"I would never away," said Poh seh tan. "I like having you in my house."

"You have a delightful house," said Tazbah. "It will be the dwelling of our delight. The God of Dawn must see to our love for I am your soft possession, your corn pollen. The ancients will make our presence delightful." She put her arms around him. "I want you before me, behind me, around me, below me, above me. All will be ecstasy until our love has felt every hue of the rainbow."

The house became a field of flowers for Tazbah and Poh seh tan. The rainbow of their love colored the flowers in all the ecstatic hues of oneness. The rich brown Earth Mother became luxuriant, gentle breezes swayed large and tiny flowers alike, birds sang in the starshine, and love was vibrantly alive, throbbing with the strength of the gentle gods. Tazbah's eyes would become as soft as the light of the Moon God but at times they would smoulder until they flashed like an erupting volcano, only to become moon splashings afterward . . .

Tazbah heard the shrill whir of the mountain cricket as she continued the climb. There was a determined look in her dark eyes, the eyes that Poh seh tan loved so much. He had been taken by them even when they flashed with fiery emotion. *Once the two had been on top of the hill and another couple rode up and had started to climb. When they got close enough Tazbah threw rocks in their direction to stop them.*

"What are you doing?" Poh seh tan asked.

"Nobody is going to share our hill," said Tazbah in an icy voice as she threw another rock.

The people below had stopped in their tracks, talked to each other as they looked up, then the man yelled, "What are you doing?"

"Go away!" Tazbah yelled back. "This is our hill!" She hurled another stone with all her might.

The man and woman below decided to retreat. "Jealous!" yelled the man. "Crazy!" yelled the woman. But they both left the hill to Poh seh tan and Tazbah, even if the story would spread around and the promontory began to be called "the hill of the jealous one."

"Why did you do that?" asked Poh seh tan, a little smile of wonderment on his face.

"Because I love you," replied Tazbah.

"And I love you. Be calm. No one can rob us of our love."

Tazbah slipped on a rock but she caught herself with her hands before any serious damage was done. The hot rock made her recoil back to her feet. She rubbed them softly on her clothes but the heat had been so intense she thought she would blister as she looked at her finger tips.

"I don't want you to get blisters on your hands," Poh seh tan had admonished her. "You do not have to work in the fields. I will do that on my own."

"But I want to be with you," Tazbah had said. "I cannot bear the sorrow when I do not see you. Besides, among my people the fields belong to the women. Men are warriors. The fields are women's work."

"Our customs are different," said Poh seh tan. "Go to the house and I will see you this afternoon."

"You put me out of your workshop, now you do not want me in your fields?" demanded Tazbah.

"I love you my dearest, calm yourself."

"How can you love me and not wish to be with me?"

"You are my wish," said Poh seh tan. "You know that we must work also. I would never stop you from weaving. I need time for the fields and the jewelry. I do it for both of us, my love."

"I would never weave if I could be with you instead."

Tazbah looked up and felt a little dizzy but she was unafraid. There was the one red rock embedded in the side of the hill. The white rocks were above it, then the yellow ones. She came to the junipers with the greenish blue berries. To the side was the little tiny grotto where Poh seh tan said the wee spirits held council. She was three quarters of the way up now and still she had not seen Poh seh tan. But he loved a good joke. He would be on top, waiting to say, "What took you, my love? " Footing was really dangerous now due to the sliding shale. Tazbah couldn't shake the dizziness but she refused to afraid. A woman descended from warriors could never be conquered by fear. She continued to challenge the hill with determined force. She would show her man that he had a fearless woman. "My fierce warrior woman," Poh seh tan would say. She had to be what she was.

Tazbah came to the gray-black rock that had light green moss growing on the sunrise side. The green was beautiful on the craggy blackness as the shrill scream of the mountain cricket pierced the solitude of the hill.

"Quit your screaming," yelled Poh seh tan. "How many times do you want me to explain? I am not interested in that woman, we were just talking at the well."

"Why don't you come home and talk to me? " Tazbah yelled right back.

"I do, I always do," said Poh seh tan, trying to calm down. "Come on, let's —"

"Don't touch me! " screamed Tazbah.

"I do not want to live like this," said Poh seh tan. "I cannot."

"Then go live with her! " screamed Tazbah as she picked up a pan and hurled it at Poh seh tan, catching him full on the chest. The man staggered from the impact, then walked out of the house.

"Poh seh tan," said Tazbah from the open door, "I'm sorry, come back, please come back! "

There was just a little way to go now and Tazbah would be at the summit of the hill. The last part of the climb was the most dangerous for it was nearly straight up with ledges providing the only available footing. One slip and Tazbah would . . . but she would not allow herself to think of such things. She was descended from warriors and nothing would stop her from reaching the top and Poh seh tan. Warriors. Warriors.

"Where is the money for the bracelet? "

"I did not sell it to her," Poh seh tan had replied.

"Then where is the bracelet? " demanded Tazbah.

"I do not have it."

"Where is it? " screamed Tazbah.

"I gave it to her," yelled Poh seh tan at the top of his voice. "I am leaving you! "

"YOU GAVE IT TO HER?! " Tazbah almost seemed to be screaming a battle cry. She went to the corner where the ceremonial lance was kept, grabbed it securely, took three quick steps and hurled it at Poh seh tan with all her might. The lance struck him powerfully in the upper abdomen. Poh seh tan stood there for an instant; then a look of stark surprise came into his eyes. His mouth opened as if to speak but instead he swayed, then fell over backward.

Tazbah stood without breathing. Her eyes opened wide and the pupils closed to slits then opened to the shock of Poh seh tan on the floor. It was as if her eyes had been disconnected from her being, as if they were flashing obsidian. "AAAIIEEEEE! " Tazbah screamed like some wild mountain animal as she threw herself on Poh seh tan. She grabbed his shoulders, hugged him, kissed him, put her hands in his hair, licked his face, put her weight on him. "You must get up," she commanded. "We are warriors, you must get up!" she ordered. Her body brushed against the lance. Her face, devoid of any expression, turned to the lance and she grabbed it with both hands and pulled it out of Poh seh tan's body. The weapon dropped to the floor and Tazbah sat next to Poh seh tan the rest of the night.

Tazbah sat at the top of the hill. She saw the mountain peaks far, far away. The green junipers on the surrounding tablelands looked like tiny green mushrooms. The wind whistled through the lone cactus bush that grew amid the rocks as Johano-Ai entered his lodge in the west. The reddish light colored Tazbah's expressionless face. "Poh seh tan, Poh seh tan," murmured Tazbah. "You said you would meet me at the top of our hill. I wait in the darkness. Come to me, Poh seh tan, help me in our night journey. No sun is shining, no star is glowing. Poh seh tan, show us the path. The night is not friendly. She has closed her eyelids. The moon has forgot me and I wait in the darkness."

Tazbah sat, hardly breathing, her ears hurting from so much listening. Her eyes did not blink and none of her moved.

"Why are you sitting there when I am over here?"

Tazbah stopped breathing.

"My warrior woman, I love you."

"Poh seh tan!" gasped Tazbah. "Is that you?"

"Who else would it be on our hill? Would you not throw great boulders on any who dared come up here?"

"Where are you, Poh seh tan, show yourself to me."

"Come with me. Over here."

Tazbah stood up. "Tell me, show me. Stretch out your hand. I want to bathe my body in your soul."

"Come with me and we shall always be together, walking among the flowers of red, blue, and yellow."

"Yes, yes, yes." Try as she might, Tazbah's eyes could not see Poh seh tan. She stumbled in every direction but her eyes captured only shadows. "Poh seh tan, I will come to your love." She bent forward at the waist until long black hair hung down. She straightened up, keeping her beautiful hair in front of her face, and in three calm steps she was over the edge, plummeting to the spirit world.

IX

THE LAST PENITENTE

When Rodrigo Griego left Seboyeta he disappeared without even taking his belongings. A few months later some of the villagers decided to take his clothes and books to the university where he had been studying. On campus they found out what department Rodrigo had been working in and were told yes, Rod Griego was working on his dissertation. No, they didn't know where he was right now. Clothes and books? There were no facilities for keeping them. "Strange that Rod would leave his books. He is quite a scholar, you know." The villagers returned to Seboyeta and one of the families volunteered to keep Griego's belongings until he returned.

About a dozen years after the villagers had gone to seek Rodrigo at the university some teenagers were walking home along in front of the church. It was late at night but they stopped when they heard what appeared to be someone receiving a severe whipping. The church door proved to be locked and since nothing else appeared to be open they quickly decided to be on their way. The story aroused other people in the village but nothing was in evidence the following night. A year later someone else testified to the exact same story and another man swore he had seen someone by the cross behind the *morada*, the lodge of the Penitente Brotherhood. The next evening there were many people out but nothing happened. The Penitentes decided to piece the story together: whatever was happening inside the church occurred during the last week in August. The exact day was unknown. When the activity in the church was finished something or somebody visited the morada. They resolved to investigate the matter once and for all.

The following August found the Penitente Brotherhood out in full force during the last week of the month. The villagers cooperated in not becoming curiosity-seekers, confident that the Brotherhood would find out whatever there was to learn. Two Brothers kept a vigil every night of the week. On Friday, a little after midnight, the Penitente flute was heard calling the Brotherhood to assemble at the church. Forewarned and prepared, the Brothers of Light arrived on the scene within a few minutes. The Elder Brother unlocked the church door and all entered. The *swish-splat* of the whip echoed throughout the church. It appeared to be coming from the choir loft directly above the group. Between the sounds of the lash there seemed to be the muffled sobs of contrition. The Elder Brother motioned for everyone to go outside and the Brotherhood obeyed.

"Perhaps we should not disturb the penance. It might be a soul trying to get out of Purgatory."

"What if he needs our help?" someone asked. "It would be our duty to help him into salvation."

The penance was becoming more and more severe as the men talked softly. One man, Aurelio, volunteered to ascend the choir loft and was given permission to do so. Armed with a candle and matches Aurelio entered the church, lit his candle and slowly made his way up the narrow stairway to the choir loft. The candle light shook as Aurelio trembled to the top of the stairs. The brave Penitente saw a man, or at least the figure of a man, flogging himself severely. The figure turned ever so slowly and looked at Aurelio. His eyes appeared glassy or watery as he approached Aurelio and gently touched the candle flame with the palm of his hand. Aurelio's breathing became more of a gasp as he retreated halfway down the stairs, re-lit the candle and once more made his way to the top of the stairs. Again the figure stopped his merciless scourging and approached Aurelio who saw him clearly for an instant until the hand again snuffed out the candle light. Aurelio retreated for the last time. His courage failed him or he felt his presence was not wanted for he left the church and informed the Brothers of what had happened.

"He does not need us," said the Elder Brother as he knelt to pray on the steps of the church. The others followed his example. While the Brotherhood prayed the whip became silent. The church door opened and out came the figure Aurelio had seen in the choir loft. The Brothers made the sign of the cross and did not hesitate to move out of the way. The stranger walked past them and up toward the rim of mesas which surrounded the village. He brought the whip down on his back every second step. After a short discussion the Penitentes decided to follow him. They caught up and saw the stranger's bleeding back, the body becoming visibly weak as he walked through a trail up the mesa all the way around to the other end of the village. He came down the mesa directly behind the Penitente *morada*. The stranger ended his whipping by kneeling at the cross for a few moments. He then stood with his back to the cross and extended his arms sideways to the level of his shoulders. He seemed to drift up to the cross and hang there full length until his head fell forward. Suddenly he began to fade and was gone.

The reverent, trembling Penitentes knelt and prayed for this was doubtless the soul of a dead Penitente who had not done his duty in life, a false Penitente whom God had sent back to earth in order to earn the right to enter Heaven.

There were some who believed Rodrigo Griego had something to do with all these happenings. It was recounted how Rodrigo had returned to Seboyeta.

the village of his childhood, after many long years of study at the university. He was remembered as an obedient, well mannered child and welcomed after his long absence. He still had some distant relatives in Seboyeta and was especially close to his grandfather's youngest brother, a man known as Tata Lito for his age and experience. Tata Lito had been Elder Brother, the *Hermano Mayor,* of the Penitente Brotherhood when it was the strongest type of organization in the mountain villages. Rodrigo wanted to tell the inside story of the Penitentes. He had to write a dissertation for his Ph.D. studies so he rented a house in Seboyeta and turned to Tata Lito for help.

"Tata," Rodrigo would say at the beginning, "I have to tell the story of the Penitentes as they really were. Many outsiders have come in and given us all a bad name. They say the Brotherhood is a collection of fanatics who sin all year long, then try to repent for three days at Easter. They say Penitentes are like the Ku Klux Klan."

"Está bien," replied Tata Lito. "What is the KluKlu . . . how? " Rodrigo explained the essentials. "No, we aren't KluKlus." The elderly man sitting on the porch of his home seemed to blend with the shadows of dusk and twilight. Only within the last couple of decades had the white crept into his hair. The years had begun to burden him though they had never ravaged his body. Of late he preferred the shade to the sun, the sunset to the sunrise. He still enjoyed a leisurely stroll through the village, frequently visiting the church, but he also found great satisfaction merely sitting on his front porch. Passersby would greet him with an affectionate, *"Buenas noches, don Manuel. ¿Cómo se siente? "* and the younger generation would chirp *"Buenas noches, Tata Lito."* To all he would wish a good evening and to inquiries of his health he would say he was feeling well, which was not always true. Though he had outlived most of his friends and was perhaps a little lonely he never expressed it. If dying ever entered his mind he never talked about it. He belonged to Seboyeta: it was his and he was a part of everyone.

Rodrigo scrutinized his relative as he gazed around the village nestled into the horseshoe rim of mountains. He could see the fertile plots of farm land below, the terraced sides of the mountains so full of tall, clinging shapes above. The land gave sustenance while the mountains seemed to yield the harvest of permanence. The moonlight splashed its softness on the mountain rim, the mesas, then the tin roofs and earth colored adobe. Part of Tata Lito's body was shaded by the porch while his hands, laying peacefully on his thighs and seldom used to gesture, caught Rodrigo's full attention: the veins were large, the fingernails thick, the skin the color of Earth Mother. Strong hands they must have been and gentle enough to nestle an infant to his heart. Rodrigo reacted by looking at his own academic hands and fingers, then turned back to those of Tata Lito, *don* Manuel. How many *vigas,* how many timber beams had he put on houses during his lifetime? How many tears had those enduring hands wiped away from weeping eyes? How often had they turned the pages of the Penitente psalm book? Had they struggled with the cross to Calvary? Had they hung limp for a crucifixion?

HEARTLAND

"No importa," repeated Tata Lito, "it does not matter if outsiders do not understand us. Penitentes are imperfect men like the rest of humanity."

"But we have to tell the story so that good people will know us as we really are and were, not as our enemies would have them believe." Rodrigo was being sincere as well as practical. He wanted to write an authentic account as well as fulfill requirements for his degree.

Tata Lito merely nodded slightly and the younger man did not press it directly. "I know much about the Brotherhood is secret. I don't want you to tell me any of that, believe me, Tata. All I want is for people to know things the way you know and feel them." He changed the subject. "Will there be enough water for the crops this year? " ·

"God willing. This June has been a bit dry though we had a couple of good rains last month."

It was July before the subject of Penitentes was brought up again. Rodrigo really didn't want to force his Tata into anything. He had spent much time working in the elderly man's garden and orchard while he gathered bits and pieces of Penitente information from other villagers. Tata Lito was not unaware of the interesting notes compiled by Rodrigo and *el viejito* must have come to admire the scholar's discipline and sense of mission, for one day he offered to take him for a walk which wound up at the *morada*. Perhaps the older man's sense of posterity had been awakened, perhaps he just wanted to help.

The key was applied to the lock on the door and Tata Lito creaked it open. Rodrigo's eyes saw nothing until they became accustomed to the scant light that entered through the open door. He became aware of a nervousness, a sense of foreboding as the former Elder Brother closed the door and struck a match to light a kerosene lamp. The match exploded into life, almost disappeared, then settled into a steady flame as Tata removed the glass chimney and lit the wick. The room was bathed in soft amber lamplight. Rodrigo was slightly startled to see a full sized image of a crucified Christ hanging on the wall. His hands and feet were nailed to the Cross, blood was flowing from His wounds.

"This is our *morada,"* stated Tata Lito, unaware of his relative's reactions.

"Cuántos . . . how many Penitentes are there in Seboyeta? "

"Sixteen."

"Do you still hold services? "

"Sí."

Rodrigo was hesitant to ask him about crucifixions. Instead he decided to let Tata Lito say what he wished when he wished. He studied the room in an effort to imprint everything in his mind since he had neither paper nor pencil. On one side of the room there was an altar filled with *santos,* hand carved images of saints, and candles in little red jars. On another wall there was a full-sized painting of the Holy Virgin Mary. Along the walls of the room were pews which perhaps had been donated by the church. Suddenly the air was pierced with what might have been described as the wail of some unearthly spirit. Rodrigo was momentarily shaken by the strains of the *pito,* the Penitente flute used to call the faithful. After his initial discomfort he saw Tata

Lito had gone through a small door in the corner of the chapel, that the simple yet torturing melody emanated from the unlighted blackness. Rodrigo went to the doorway and hesitated. "Tata? "

"*Sí, hijo.* Bring the lamp."

After fetching the light Rodrigo made his way into the smaller room to find a variety of Penitente paraphernalia as well as various tools like shovels, picks, etc., even a saddle. There was a large cross which ran almost the entire length of the room. A man could easily fit on it. In one corner was an assortment of heavy chains but his attention was completely captured by the cart of Death. The small wagon appeared to be ancient: wheels of solid wood, no nails in evidence, no iron parts of any kind. The death figure was enough to strike terror into anyone for it was a skeleton clothed in a black dress. The eyes of the figure were some sort of black stone which caught the light of the lamp and returned it in an eerie fashion, almost as if it was scrutinizing Rodrigo, watching him, questioning, wondering.

"Only Penitentes are allowed in here," said Tata Lito in a low voice. "You must never . . ." He didn't finish but the sound of the human voice was enough to break the hypnotic spell which Death had cast on Rodrigo.

"What? " asked the younger man as he psychologically pulled away from the Death figure, thus enabling himself to perceive other items in the cart: the bow and arrow Death held in hand, the crude axe and club behind the figure. Then he noticed the whips, three of them, hanging on the wall to the left of the cart. Completely engrossed and without speaking he took one from its place and inspected: it was about three feet long and weighed maybe a couple of pounds. From his previous studies he knew the whip was made of the yucca plant fibers. He grasped the braided handle with both hands and swung it vigorously over his right shoulder. The pain came as a shock for there was nothing academic about it. His shirt was scant protection for the five inch width of whip which stung him, feeling much like the vigorous swish of a horse's tail. Tata Lito put his hand on the whip.

"Only for penance, *hijo.*" Rodrigo respected his Tata's wishes and placed the whip back on the wall.

"They say Penitentes are brothers of the lash," commented Rodrigo as he gazed at the whips.

"No, they are wrong. We are first of all brothers, then we are brothers in penance. The whip is a penance, nothing more. We are ordinary people who know one must earn salvation."

"They say the Brotherhood is the cult of death."

"No. We are *Hermanos de Luz,* Brothers of Light who show the way. Life is suffering and death for *Jesucristo* died on the cross for us all. He didn't have to, he chose to. We don't have to do penances, we choose to."

"They would tell us," continued Rodrigo, "that it is not necessary to bleed so much for salvation."

"I hope they are right," said the old man.

Rodrigo realized that Tata Lito was not interested in academic argument or defense. "Tata, how old were you when you became a Penitente? " He looked about the room for other items.

"I don't know, about sixteen, seventeen, thereabouts."

Rodrigo took down from its place on a hook in the wall what appeared to be a black bag. In his hands he recognized it as the head bag worn by the man being crucified during Easter ritual. "Did most teenagers become Penitentes? "

"No, not everyone."

"About half? "

"A little less."

Rodrigo replaced the head bag on its hook. "Whose lantern is this? "

"Everything here belongs to the Brotherhood."

"Donated? "

"Bought. We buy everything we own."

"You mean the Brotherhood owns things outright? " asked Rodrigo.

"Yes. We bought this building. We own sheep, cattle, and a few horses. We pay the woodcarver for new santos. We help members of the Brotherhood when they are in need. We donate money to the church and sometimes for things the town needs."

"Those are the Penitentes nobody knows," exclaimed Rodrigo with enthusiasm. "They think everything is sensationalism." He noted the several small crucifixes, suitable for carrying during processions.

Tata Lito shrugged. "We do penances, we help our brothers, we pray. More than anything else we pray for that is our basic belief. We try to imitate the life of Christ, including his suffering, for we believe we were created in His image. Earthly pain is nothing compared to eternity."

Rodrigo went over to a small table on which were placed two *matracas,* the ratchet-like noise makers used to give signals during processions. There was also a worn volume which turned out to contain *alabados,* psalms and prayers used during Penitente ceremonies.

"We must be going," said Tata Lito. He motioned for Rodrigo to take the lamp back into the chapel. Rodrigo did so, carefully hiding his reluctance. He replaced the lamp on the altar, knelt down alongside Tata Lito who was already praying. The two men remained for a few minutes then made the sign of the cross and got back on their feet. Tata went to the crucifix, kissed the feet of the crucified Christ then returned to blow out the light. Only when the chapel was bathed in darkness did Rodrigo notice there was not a window in any of the walls. Shadows made by the gilded lamp light had completely taken over until Tata Lito opened the door. Moonlight arrived in the shape of a rectangle, two human shadows crowded out some moonlight, then a creaking door allowed solitude to reign supreme.

Tata Lito waited for Rodrigo as the scholar turned to look at the *morada* from a few yards away. Its only distinguishing feature was a small cross on the roof directly over the doorway. Otherwise it was merely another adobe building in the village. The two men walked the length of the village to visit the church, then parted for the night.

The two men spent most of their days together the rest of the summer and each came to understand the other. The old man's health did not seem to improve but the scholar filled his notebooks with Penitente information as seen by an insider. Rodrigo found some of the facts hard to believe but mostly he was awed by the religious sense of the Penitentes. They returned to the *morada* several times and on one occasion they went behind the building to inspect the crosses kept there. Rodrigo tried to lift one to his shoulder and barely succeeded. "How can they drag this in a procession?" he groaned, straining under the weight as he pulled it away from the wall against which it had rested. He managed to drag it a few yards then let it down before it crashed down on him. Rodrigo caught his breath and asked, "Tata, what does it feel like to be . . . crucified?" There was no answer. "You have taken the agonies of Christ?" The *viejito* nodded. "What does it feel like?" The evening silence was broken only by Rodrigo's heavy breathing. He went into the back room of the lodge and emerged with a shovel whereupon he started digging a deep, narrow hole. The scholar was oblivious to the night and everything in it until he had finished. Rodrigo then strained until he was able to put the cross in the hole, replacing some of the dirt to make it firm. The cross was at least seven feet high and could easily support the weight of a man.

"Tata, I want you to help me."

"No, that would be sacrilege."

"*Por favor,*" implored Rodrigo, "this one last thing. You won't have to do anything except help me down. *Please,* Tata." Rodrigo went into the *morada* again and returned with two lengths of rope and a chair. His breath came quickly as he made loops of the rope and put them through the arms of the cross until they were almost the width of his shoulders. He placed the chair next to the sturdy timber pointing toward the heavens, stood on the wobbling chair as he turned his back against the cross, then turned the loops a few times and inserted his arms as far as he could go. Rodrigo took a deep breath, then pushed the chair out from under him.

At first he thought his arms would slip out all the way but the rope caught and held tightly around his elbows. His first impression was the pressure of the ropes on his skin. Within short seconds he was aware of an agonizing pull on his shoulders, as if his bones were coming out of socket. He began to lose track of time as the flesh on his chest seemed to tear with the pressure. His breathing became a gulp. Rodrigo frantically moved his head every which way in an effort to get air. He even pushed against the wood in order to loosen himself. He became aware of a crunching throb in the small of his back. The bite of the rope was gone. He knew only that he couldn't breathe, that pain was master in the marrow of his bones. His head began to fall forward when he uttered, "Tata . . . help me . . . the chair."

Tata Lito had been trance-like until Rodrigo's plea reached him. He sprang for the chair, placing it against the cross as he tried to put Rodrigo's feet on it. He got up on the chair and lifted his relative to relieve the pressure on his lungs. "Step on the back of the chair and work your arms out," ordered the older man. He realized he couldn't work on the ropes and hold the body up at the same time. "Breathe in . . . deeply."

HEARTLAND

Rodrigo heard the voice as from a distance. He was nearly within the realm of an unconscious world made up of all the contrasting colors of the spectrum. He felt his soul being lifted to the mountain top where the air was crisp and pure. He stepped back from the brink, the precipice, the glimpse of eternity.

"Breathe in," a voice counseled him. "Breathe in deeply and pull an arm out of the rope."

He became aware of being lifted as he struggled with the rope around his right arm. He panicked when he thought he would be unable to extricate himself, then he felt it slide past his elbow and down his forearm. Once his right arm was free the other was no problem: Rodrigo nearly crumpled to the ground right on top of Tata Lito, yet the old man held him until both were sitting on the ground.

"*Dios mío,*" sighed Rodrigo as he grimaced.

"May the Lord have mercy," said Tata Lito. "The fault was mine."

"Nonsense, I did it of my own free will. There is no one to blame but myself. Thank God nothing serious came of it." Rodrigo looked at Tata and noticed a strange vitality exuding from the old man, quite a contrast to his own physical condition. "Come on, I'll walk home with you." He wanted to get his impressions down on paper while they were still fresh in his mind.

"You go ahead. I want to pray in the chapel."

Rodrigo asked him if he was certain he could get back alone even though it appeared Rodrigo would need help before Tata Lito did.

"Yes, I will be fine. You go on." The two men walked into the *morada* and Rodrigo exited out the front door, closing it softly behind him. He heard Tata Lito's voice in prayer: "*Venir pecadores, venir con su cruz, adorar la sangre del dulce Jesús...*" Rodrigo hurried to his house and worked to record his impressions as exactly as possible. Completely fatigued when he finally finished he stumbled off to bed where he slept deeply until he started dreaming. Just before he woke up he dreamed he was in the *morada,* a full fledged member of the Penitente Brotherhood. The group had just crucified one of its members and Rodrigo was helping to get him off the cross. He became very anxious when he could not unfasten the knots which bound the crucified man's limbs to the cross. He called the other Brothers to help then went to his notes on the Penitentes to see if he had something written down on how to untie Penitente knots. His notebooks were covered with the dust of disuse and when he opened one it crumbled in his hands. He returned to help but the Brotherhood had untied the knots. Rodrigo jumped to take the individual off the cross but he couldn't budge the man. It seemed the Brother's arms and legs were still bound. Then he saw the nails through the palm's of the Penitente's hands, the nails through his feet. Rodrigo called out for help but he found himself completely alone with the work of the crucifixion, the bleeding man on the cross. He noticed the blood on his own palms and something made him reach over to remove the hood from the head of the crucified Brother. He saw himself staring at his own face...

Rodrigo awoke with a start. Thank goodness it had only been a dream! As he sat up in bed he became aware of an excruciating soreness in his shoulders.

He lay limp for a few minutes then forced himself to get up and dress. Academic life had disciplined his mind though it hadn't done much for his body, he thought ruefully as he massaged one shoulder, then the other. He felt better when he went over his notes. He became elated when he envisioned the Ph.D. disseration that would come from them. His rising enthusiasm wouldn't contain itself so he briskly walked in the direction of Tata Lito's home to share his elation. Mornings in Seboyeta during the last days of August are crisp and invigorating, foretelling the colorful autumn season of change. All seasons sweet, but amber-hued autumn best of all, exhilarated Rodrigo as he arrived at his Tata's home. He knocked on the door . . . no answer . . . so he opened it.

"Buenos días le de Dios, Tata Lito," he said. Tata was no where to be seen. "Maybe the back porch," Rodrigo mumbled to himself . . . no, not there either. He went into the bedroom and saw the bed hadn't been slept in. His elation began to . . . *"What if he fell on the way home last night? ! "* He hurried out of the house and ran as fast as he could toward the *morada.* The villagers looked at him in wonderment as he flew past them. The scholar appeared so harried a couple of the men followed him to see if he was all right.

Rodrigo threw his full weight against the door of the *morada* and burst it open. The peaceful lamp light contrasted the gasping of Rodrigo's need for air as his eyes focused to the chapel light. Under the crucified Christ was Tata Lito.

"Tata, wake up, it is morning," sighed a relieved Rodrigo. He touched the old man. "Tata? . . . Tata . . . no . . ." A whip lay beside the old man whose eyes stared into eternity.

We do penances, we help our brothers, we pray.

"God in heaven, NO," sobbed Rodrigo as he embraced Tata Lito.

We try to imitate the life of Christ . . .

X

IDYLLS

The creaky ride to Santa Fe was spent in leisurely chuckles and conversation between Lorenzo and Santiago while they gazed at the mountain beauty which is northern New Mexico.

"... so when the man was elected President he wanted to know more about this part of the country. He sent a gentleman to travel around the territories and make a report. This man wrote down all his impressions and time was running out in September when he got to New Mexico so he hurried his trip but he really liked northern New Mexico so he spent a few extra days travelling through our mountains though he didn't have time to talk to the people. *Bueno,* when he got back to Washington he made his report and down at the end there was a note saying, 'The mountain people of New Mexico seem to be very religious.' The President didn't know exactly what to make of it so he asked the man what it meant.

'Yes, when I went through northern New Mexico I saw many people praying in the mountains.'

'Praying in the mountains? You mean they have many churches there? '

'No, I saw them kneeling under the trees.'

'Hmmm,' said the President, but he didn't understand.

"Well, the story got around and finally one of our people who worked in those offices heard about it. He made an appointment with the President and when he got in to see him he told him:

'I guess our Raza are as religious as most people,' explained the New Mexican, 'but the people weren't praying in the mountains.'

'Oh, what were they doing under the trees? '

'They were picking piñon nuts.'

Santiago Montoya and Lorenzo Ochoa were more like brothers than distant in-laws. When they had married sisters some thirty-odd years ago, thus becoming *concuños,* they came to realize they had many things in common and over the years they had become brothers in all positive aspects. They had

HEARTLAND

formed a partnership in a sheep shearing business and their *concuño* relationship was greatly respected by the villagers of their native Peñasco for if Lorenzo and Santiago ever had any battles such as business partners are prone to have no one heard of them. Apart from their seasonal shearing business, *los concuños,* as the villagers affectionately referred to them, had their farms and enviable reputations for other abilities. Santiago was a recognized musician, much in demand for singing, playing the violin or the guitar for dances. Lorenzo was the acknowledged poet of Peñasco and not unknown in the rest of the north. The talents of one complemented those of the other for Lorenzo could write an *alabado* prayer or a *corrido* epic poem and Santiago could set it to music.

Montoya was a tall man, robust, with the set jaw of a man of the earth. His voice was deep whether booming in song or good natured laughter. Ochoa was not as tall, not as outgoing as his *hermano* Santiago. Lorenzo's hands were accustomed to hard work yet the fingers were long and slender. The faces of both men were lined by sun, wind, and mountain yet there was warmth in the eyes, a softness that comes of permanence, of acquiescence to Nature, of being at peace with the earth, of humility before God.

"Mírate para allá. Look ye over there," Santiago told Lorenzo amid chuckles over his own story. Up ahead of their wagon there had been a noon rain which had lasted just long enough to give added life to the mountains. The newly emerging noonday sun was slanting down the rocky slopes, lighting the masses of evergreens penetrated with rain. Far into the recesses of the valley green vistas arched like hollows of mighty waves of some eternal ocean. Mist began to rise from the canyons and seemingly float toward the men in the wagon. It unveiled the winding valleys and couched in quiet iridescent masses which sunlight converted in rainbow hues. The mist faded away, lost in lustre, then appeared again in a heaven serene like a bright, impossible dream, foundationless and inaccessible.

"How do you paint a soul?" almost whispered Lorenzo.

"Quien sabe," uttered Santiago.

Sometime after the shearing season and before crops were ready to be harvested the *concuños* were accustomed to hitching up the horses and travelling to Santa Fe in order to purchase a ten gallon keg of whiskey. While the two men liked their cups as well as anyone the venture was more business than pleasure. It was an investment which they would retail by the drink in plazas of the outlying villages. On this day, before setting out, they had made a solemn pledge not to give the other any of the whiskey intended for sale.

Upon arriving in Santa Fe later that afternoon the purchase of the keg was arranged for. When it was agreed upon that the whiskey would be picked up the following morning the *concuños* went to the plaza to shop for gifts to give their wives and grandchildren. Marcia, Lorenzo's wife, was very fond of turquoise jewelry. Mercedes, Santiago's woman-love, couldn't resist a beautifully woven blanket. The markets were almost ready to close down though one could see the varieties of meats, fruits, vegetables, brought to town by the country people. There was mutton, pork, and beef hung up on lines between

110

posts of the portals. Seasonal vegetables and fruits were placed on little mats or pieces of boards on the ground. Here was a covered basket full of bread baked that morning, there was a family selling milk and cheese. Some Indians were selling venison, dried as well as fresh. Wild turkeys were also for sale and on this day there was even some bear meat.

"*Amigo,*" said Lorenzo to the Indian selling venison, "how is it going? "

The man nodded at first then talked quite freely in Spanish. Most of the fresh meat had been sold but he still had some dried.

"I will buy some *carne seca,*" commented Lorenzo, "then I would like for you to do me a favor." He explained that he wanted to buy some turquoise and a blanket for his wife, that he wanted the meat man to help him arrive at a fair price, that he would give him something for his services.

"*Bueno,*" said the Indian without hesitating. "You tell me what you want and I will get you the best price." The *concuños* told the man they would return to tell him what items they wanted and from whom. After strolling among the jewelers and weavers, seeing what they wanted yet pretending disinterest, they returned to the meat man. The poet from Peñasco indicated a desire to buy a certain delicate bracelet of silver and turquoise. The musician was interested in a three-by-five rug with alternating colors of orange, brown, and black. All three men went to the booths where the desired items were, Lorenzo asking the price of the rug, Santiago inquiring the same about the bracelet. Later the Indian said, "The rug is Navajo, the bracelet Zuni, and I am a Taos but I will see what I can do. Come back tomorrow morning."

"*Buenas noches,*" said Santiago as he and Lorenzo headed toward their wagon. They drove to the house of Filomeno García and knocked on the large door which was beautifully hand carved.

"*¿Quién es?* " from within. A dog begins to bark.

"*Amigos.*"

The door is opened sufficiently to see who it is then recognition and old friendships burst it wide. "Don Santiago, Don Lorenzo, *pasen!* Come in, come in! Rumalda, look who is here! " The aroma of supper cooking on the stove, an enticing fragrance of meat, chile, and tortillas, is as delicious as the embraces of friendships for the men are *compadres.* There is a vertible melee of hugs and handshakes as grandchildren are reintroduced and a cat escapes from a child's arms only to get stepped on.

"Put the cat outside, *hijito,*" cautions Don Filomeno. "What are you doing in Santa Fe? Come sit down."

"The dog," reminds the grandchild.

"Of course you will have supper and stay the night."

"Our yearly investment," smiles Lorenzo.

"And how are Doña Marcia and Doña Mercedes? " inquires Doña Rumalda.

Supper was most pleasing and after seeing to the horses the evening was spent in the conversation of reminiscence. Everyone slept well that night and before the sun was very high the next morning the men breakfasted and were ready to attend to business. The Garcías promised to go spend a few days in Peñasco and *los concuños* promised to return quickly.

HEARTLAND

"*Vuelvan.* Come back soon."

"*Lleguen.* Come see us soon."

The men went to pick up their keg of whiskey, paid for it and had it loaded and tied down properly in the wagon. They patted the keg, took a deep whiff of the scent and remembered their pledge not to give the other a drop of the aromatic liquid. Their first stop was the plaza where they found the Taos Indian who informed them about the items they wished to buy.

"Too expensive," sighed Lorenzo in convincing fashion. "Let us buy some carne seca for the trip home." He decided how much he wanted then asked the seller if he wanted money or a trade.

"What do you have to trade? "

Santiago strolled over to the wagon and poured the man a drink.

"This is not a sale," remarked Santiago, "this is a gift for you."

The Taos decided to trade his sale for whiskey instead of money. Santiago poured out the agreed upon amount into the Taos' glittering clay jar. On the way back to his meat stand he passed by the jeweler and weaver, informing them that a good trade might be possible. The men came to see Lorenzo and Santiago, each asked which items they were interested in and returned to see if they still had them. They did, so they drove the best possible bargain, the jeweler receiving a gallon and a half of whiskey for his bracelet, the weaver getting a little over a gallon for the blanket. Marcia and Mercedes would be just as happy as the present buyers and sellers.

"I will buy you *un traguito,*" offered Santiago as he poured one each for the men.

"*Muchas gracias, caballero.*"

The *concuños* purchased some toys for their grandchildren, placed all the gifts in a secure area under the driver's seat then headed out of town to see how business was in the villages to the north. They drove for a couple of hours, passing Camel Rock and the countless eroded formations in the sandstone capped hills which were a prelude to forest pines. The first village on the itinerary was Cuyamungue, a settlement of adobe houses whose walls would soon be clustered with *ristras,* strings of red chile. With the Jemez and Sangre de Cristo mountains in the blue distance, the green fields of alfalfa and small orchards of Cuyamungue had an air of welcome as the wagon made its way to the center of the tiny village.

"*Hermano,* would you care for a drinklet today? " asked Lorenzo of a man carrying a shovel.

"How much? "

"Ten cents. Good whiskey from Santa Fe."

"A little expensive but let me try one."

Others came to the wagon and enjoyed a drink or two. When business came to a standstill Lorenzo and Santiago lingered around the spout of the keg for a second or two then quickly got into the wagon and moved on toward Pojoaque. There was more scenery than people on the road along this rolling desert strip with its miniature canyons, cliffs, mesas, and multi-colored layers of rock. The exposed sandy river beds were dry so crossing was not hazardous this day.

"I am a little dry," remarked Santiago as he looked at the sands. "Maybe you could sell me a drink."

"Remember your promise," reminded Lorenzo, who wanted one just as badly.

"We promised not to *give* each other a drink. I want to *buy* one."

"You have money? " teased Lorenzo.

"I have money, good credit, and an honest face."

"I don't know about the face."

"You know, the ugliest face I ever saw, I mean *really* ugly ... I think Nature committed a sin when that poor lady got her face ... I was still in my teens, travelling around, and I happened to stop by the well where this lady was getting water. I got down from my horse and asked if I could have some water. She said sure and handed me her gourd. Then I saw her face and even my horse turned away. I didn't know what side of the gourd she had been drinking from and I sure didn't want to put my lips where she had put hers. She just looked at me as I turned the gourd this way and that. I decided the edge furthest from the handle would be safer than either of the sides so I drank up.

"You do me honor by drinking from the same spot I do, young man," said the old lady as she smiled, showing her toothless gums. ¡*Caramba*! I jumped on my horse and threw my face into the first stream I found."

The sun was setting when the wagon and its occupants arrived in the adobe village of Santa Cruz. As luck would have it there was going to be a wedding the next morning so the plaza was busier than usual. *Concuño* enterprise did its best to contribute to the merriment.

"¿*Un traguito*? ¡*Cómo no*! A drinklet? Why not! " seemed to be the only enchantment needed. Santiago was worried they might sell out their entire stock but finally sales died down to a trickle.

"Let us go see my *primo hermano*," said Lorenzo as the last of the coins were deposited in the wagon seat which would have to be dismantled in order to take them out. At the home of Salvador Sánchez, Lorenzo's first cousin, the two men were greeted with jubilation and affection amid the "What are you doing in Santa Cruz? ... Come, supper is ready ... Of course you will stay with us tonight ..."

Doña Carlota, Salvador's wife, was quite talented in the kitchen according to the dictates of tradition. She was also well known for her ability with growing flowers and her home was a veritable spectrum of color, the pride of her family and neighborhood. She loved her flowers and they responded to her care. "How goes it with the flowers? " was all anyone had to ask to get a guided tour of her yard, garden, and home:

"My white carnations are jealous of my red ones ... maybe because the reds get the morning sun first. Oh, these geraniums are too strong for any of the flowers except the hollyhocks. Santiago, you must sing us some songs tonight for my red roses become richer in color when they hear pretty music . . ."

"Of course," agreed Santiago.

Supper consisted of newly baked bread topped with homemade butter, *frijoles* and *temole,* sweet rice for dessert. After some coffee a guitar was brought out and everyone went into the back yard to enjoy hearing Santiago sing the evening away:

> The humming bird tells me
> Not to be looking for love
> But to continue as she does
> Sipping the flowers . . .

The comical *Don Simón:*

> In my times the women dressed with moderation,
> Their dresses well pinned at the collar,
> And their skirts touched the heels of their shoes . . .

And love songs like *Morena:*

> My dark haired love
> Have you ever really
> Been in love?
> Yes, 'cause in your soul
> Lives tranquility.
>
> You have planted a vine below your window,
> One that clings to your balcony;
> Every time I pass by your house I tell myself,
> There lives the owner of my love . . .

The following morning Lorenzo and Santiago were fortified with a hearty breakfast of *huevos rancheros,* hitched up the horses and departed amid the chorus of

"*Vuelvan,*"

"*Lleguen,*"

as they headed east toward Chimayo.

The narrow Santa Cruz Valley was producing its fields of corn, chile, pinto beans, orchards laden with apples and peaches. The sides of the valley were walled by sandstone cliffs carved by Nature while below a rock-strewn stream curved its way hither and yon without interference from man. Adobe houses nestled against tawny cliffs or perched on hilltops. Young children in joyous freedom played by the roadside and stared at passers-by from behind curious, laughing eyes.

The village of Chimayo was the first stop that morning. The road winding through the village was lined with lilac hedges, patio walls, adobe houses. Santiago reined the horses to a stop in the center of town and was greeted by name.

"*¿Un traguito?* "

"*Cómo no,*" and business had started.

"And what can you tell me about the Christ Child?" asked Lorenzo of one of his customers.

"I bought him a pair of new shoes last Christmas," replied the man, referring to the popular belief that the *Santo Niño* would wear out his shoes from going out to play games with the children of the poor. El Santuario de Chimayo, the famous sanctuary, was a living part of the villagers life and piety.

Court was in session and Augustín Chávez related the story of how his brother was on the witness stand. The prosecuting attorney asked him how many children he had.

"*Once.* Eleven."

"*¡Once!* " exclaimed the prosecutor in no slight wonderment. "*¿Todos vivos?* "

"*Unos vivos, otros tontos, pero todos comen.*"

The judge ordered a fifteen minute recess so that everyone could regain a composure more fitting in a court of law.

"*Hombre,* you *señores* aren't drinking," commented one of the customers to the bartenders. "Here, let me buy you each a drinklet."

Before Santiago could protest the coins were in his hand. "The bartender shouldn't drink," cautioned Lorenzo as he watched the coins in Santiago's possession.

"*Anda.* Go on," said another customer. The two thus found themselves with drinks in their hands and wondered how they could get themselves out of the predicament. Santiago took a whiff of the liquor, shook his head, then drank the whiskey. Lorenzo's resistance melted with that of his friend: he tilted his head back as the glass reached his lips. It was the first whiskey the two had tasted and so good that everyone in the group was treated to a drink on the house.

When business died down the whiskey wagon headed for Cundiyo, a tiny village where there had been a funeral that morning. Santiago traded some whiskey for a young goat to take to his grandson Pablo but there were no drinks sold or attempted. Truchas Peak was in the distance as the wagon headed for the hamlet of Córdova. This mountain paradise kindled poetic fires in Lorenzo Ochoa. The mountains, the mountains . . . cathedrals of the Earth, brooding on things eternal . . . the breeze through the evergreens was an eternal hymn of praise. Perhaps eternity was the large unbroken spaces of pure violet and purple which grew deeper in the distance. Films of clouds were passing over the darkness of forest and valley, producing a saintly azure and purple which passed into rose-color delicacy in the upper summits.

The narrow road made its way across low spurs of hills and lead into Córdova with its adobe houses of pink, blue, and yellow portals which contrasted with the light green wheat fields and vivid green alfalfa. Wild plums grew along the stream that came down from the foothills and towering mountain.

"We must remember our pledge this time," cautioned Santiago as they left the wagon to prepare for business.

"Yes," agreed Lorenzo as he took the baby goat out of the wagon and tethered it to a wheel. The bleating goat attracted attention sooner than usual and in a short while sales were going well. The men were invited to stay in the village but for some reason they chose to drive toward Truchas after being treated to a couple of drinks. While on the road they decided to stop at a clearing to gaze at Truchas Peak and drink from the cool mountain stream which babbled nearby. The animals were unhitched and allowed to drink after which they grazed at their leisure.

"Here," said Lorenzo as he handed Santiago a quarter. "I will buy you a drinklet." He poured the drink and handed it away.

"But . . .," stammered the musician, "that is not right . . . you have paid too much. I will give you a free drink in change . . ." And that was how it went. Moonlight tiptoed into the kingdom of evergreens, bathing forest spirits, gently folding flowers for a night of dreams. The trees had seemed to hush in expectation of the rising moon which shed its splendor across the dusk of early evening. Santiago and Lorenzo, engaged in conversation, heeded not the welcome as the trees wrote their approval far along the ground.

"Jack is a good gringo," Lorenzo was saying, "so when he came to the house to go see about the job I said okay, saddled the horse, and we set out. We had to ride through town so when we passed in front of the church I made the sign of the cross.

'Why do you do that? ' says Jack.

'It's our custom whenever we go in front of the cross,' says I.

'You always do that? '

'Yes.'

So we're riding along but when we come to the railroad tracks he stops his horse.

'What's the matter? ' I ask him.

'Aren't you going to make the sign? ' he says, chuckling a bit. 'There's a cross by the railroad, don't you see it'

'We don't cross ourselves for railroad crosses, just for church crosses,' I tell him.

'I don't see why. They're both crosses, made outa the same material,' he says and laughs a little chuckle.

Bueno pues, when we get to the job the head man says he'll hire us but work doesn't start until the next day. We tell him okay, that we'll be back tomorrow. Next day I go to Jack's house early in the morning. He meets me and I help him saddle his horse. His wife comes out of the house and he kisses her goodbye. We ride down the road a bit and I ask him:

'How come you did that? '

'What? You mean kiss my wife? Whenever I go anywhere we always kiss each other. It's our custom. We always say goodbye that way.'

'Why don't you kiss her bottom? ' I told him.

'What? '

'Why not? It's the same material.' "

Lorenzo poured both of them another drink. "Bring the harmonica from my bag," suggested Santiago from where he sat against a tree. The poet delivered drink and instrument to the music maker then sat himself down where he could see the moon splashing its beams on the evergreen heaven of the mountain. The melodic harmonica made time stand still as Lorenzo's spirit became verdant. What was it like to be a tree, a stream, a flitting bird in a darkling wood, a raindrop, a blade of grass? It must feel good to be a tree and push deeply inside the ground so flat and nourishing ... to feel yourself so high and grasped so tightly inside ... the wind must make them come alive ever so much, making them sway back and forth, boughs arching like arms touching, whispering their delight ... and the rain trickling down must refresh them after their daily visit with sunbeams. Did they mind wearing their cold jewelry only during the winter? Probably not, for bird nests adorned them enough in other times and there were always many visits from the forest animals like squirrels and other furry, living ornaments ...

Lorenzo walked to the stream for some cool water, cupping his hands to bring the shimmering life to his mouth. He bathed his face gently, peering into the stream as it chattered over its stony ways, hushing to a babble over small pebbles, here sliding, there skipping over hazel covers of crystal. If the mountain was the cathedral of the Earth, if the wind was the symphonic poem, water had to be the soul of Nature for its clearness, its color, its calmness, the fantasy spirit of its movement. Everything created by Nature depended on this soul substance, including the man whose reflection struggled to become distinct with the light of the moon. Lorenzo understood his own insignificance as he sat back against a big rock. Man was merely another creature of Nature, no more important than the humble, cheerful grass which fed the munching horses and the young goat. Perhaps men who could make music like Santiago came close to harmony with Nature. Harmony ... a bird in flight ... it didn't matter if it was an eagle or a humming bird. Harmony ... a raindrop coasting down a blade of grass ... a rainbow in the sky ... Marcia ... trees rooting themselves in rocky mountains, reaching for sunshine, crowding down together to drink from sweet streams, dancing in the wind around mossy knolls, resting among fragrant fields ...

The poet of Peñasco was asleep and a rainbow touched his shoulder.